Searching for Juliette

Haste Ye Back

The Secret of Kendall Mountain

It's Perfectly Safe…The Rulison Matter

Trust the Magic

The Geese that Won the War

The Ghost of a Tree Remembered

The Borrowed Days

Waiting Games

Marilyn Ludwig

Zafa Publishing

Book cover and interior designed by Ellie Searl, Publishista®

ISBN-13: 9780996742276
LCCN: 2019903533

ZAFA PUBLISHING
Downers Grove, Illinois

In memory of author Lois Duncan, a favorite of mine for years and years, whom I finally met shortly before she died. This is the kind of book you used to write. I think you would have approved.

For Linda Griscom Surlak, proofreader and pal

And for Nancy.

When I have a little girl, I'll tell her I love her every day. I'll buy her designer clothes and let her fix her hair anyway she likes. She won't even wear contact lenses unless she needs them. Perhaps I'll name her Jenny or Janice—something beginning with J—and I'll warn her never to talk to strangers. Then I'll tell her what happened to me when I was ten years old.

—— Kathryn Hunter, *My Weird Story*

"YOU NAGGED ME FOR THAT book, Kitty. Now settle down and read."
"Yes, Aunt Kay," but under my breath, I added "you mean witch." I
wouldn't admit the book I'd selected at the airport newsstand was too hard.
A Stranger is Watching was the title, and Aunt Kay had become the stranger,
as far as I was concerned.

I gave up after three pages. Ignoring Aunt Kay's frown, I browsed
through *Summer Fun Mad Libs*, a going-away present from my friend Lisa.
We made the best Mad Lib stories, filled with words we'd never dare say out
loud, except quietly to each other. But we'd never play again . . . together. I
tried to figure out how to do Mad Libs alone, but it wasn't fun. My eyes filled
with tears, and my nose started to drip.

Aunt Kay handed me a tissue. "Kitty, I'd keep you if I had enough
money. Your brother is much younger and needs me more."

Ha! She'd have picked Tim anyway. Tim looked like pictures of Mother,
cute with dimples and curly hair. I was like Dad—tall, pale, and skinny. I had
his smile, too, only I'd stopped smiling.

Aunt Kay said she was going to the "powder room" and that I should
watch the luggage. "Especially the briefcase. Then you must go brush your
hair. You resemble an overgrown shrub." She laughed, maybe trying to turn
it into a joke instead of just another scolding.

I didn't answer. I liked my hair long and shaggy. I was dark and
mysterious, especially when I wore my saucer-sized sunglasses. My friends

liked me, even some of the boys did. Who cared if she didn't? "No one says powder room anymore," I muttered, but she was gone.

Aunt Kay sure had a thing about her briefcase. I lifted it. Heavy. I'd open it, but it was locked. A cheap lock, though. I rummaged through my backpack for the little key to my own suitcase. The briefcase opened on my first try. Might as well see what I was guarding.

I opened it. Then slammed it shut—fast! Money! Lots of money! Too much money! I peeked inside again. Hundreds, I bet—maybe thousands of dollars. Only banks had that much. Aunt Kay lied. She could take care of twenty Kittys. She just didn't want to. She didn't want me.

Suddenly I had that prickly feeling you get when you sense someone watching. I closed the briefcase, locked it, and nonchalantly looked around. A woman across the aisle quickly held a newspaper to her face. A stranger is watching, I thought. But she wasn't a scary stranger, like Aunt Kay. She was normal: short, chubby, with grayish hair tightly permed—maybe a wig—but I knew she'd been watching me. Maybe she thought I looked interesting, or even pretty.

I pulled a string from my backpack. I'd do the string tricks my dad had taught me and act like I'd never seen the woman or the money. Jacob's Ladder and Cat's Cradle—then I saw her coming toward me.

"I used to do that," she said, "but I wasn't as good as you."

Of course I knew I shouldn't talk to strangers, but she was just being friendly. And it was an airport with lots of people in it—and I was alone and lonely. "It takes practice," I said. "My dad showed me how." He would have taught her more if he hadn't died. Everyone had to die, except maybe Aunt Kay. She was so mean she'd probably live forever.

Then the woman showed me some tricks, and before long I felt like we were friends. "Your mother has been gone awhile," she said.

"Aunt," I croaked, and she raised her eyebrows.

"Your mother?"

"She died when I was little."

"Your father?"

"Car accident last month," I mumbled.

"You poor girl. So you live with your aunt?"

"No, she's sending me to some relatives I don't know—in Boston." I started sniffling.

"Would you like to come with me?" she asked quietly. "I could be your mother."

Was she nuts? Oh, where was Aunt Kay? But the woman didn't sound crazy, and she acted normal and safe. I looked into her eyes, brown and kind, and was reminded of my father. And she was asking me what *I* wanted. No one had done that since Dad died. Aunt Kay didn't want me, and probably the relatives didn't either. Tim hadn't even said goodbye. Probably Aunt Kay wasn't coming back.

I slung on my backpack, grabbed my suitcase *and* the briefcase. "I'll go with you," I said.

She offered to carry my things, but I only gave her the suitcase. I hugged the briefcase to my chest. "This was my father's," I said. "It's for my drawings." I don't know why I lied back then, but it turned out to be a good thing.

We left the airport, and I stopped being Katrina Hunter and became Kathryn Harris.

CHAPTER ONE

"**W**HOA!" I REMINDED FIREFLY, ALTHOUGH she was far too intelligent a mare not to stop at the edge of Curtain Call Gap. I gazed down at a wandering blue stream and the red rocks shaped like native warriors, guarding the ranching community of Seguro Haven, Colorado. At the edge of the valley, situated on a small foothill, stood a large white house that had been my home for almost seven years.

"Kath . . . Kathy . . ."

"Here . . ." I'd answer to Kath, Kathy or Kathryn, but never to Kat, Kit, or Kay.

"Whoa, good fella. Whoa, Dynamite," came a voice from behind me. Dynamite didn't have the brains of Firefly, although he outdid her in looks—just as Leesa Dulow, my best friend, outdid me. I grinned at her choice of horses. Leesa had her pick from a dozen gentler ones, but she chose Dynamite because he complimented *her* appearance. As one might choose shoes or a purse, Leesa picked the horse that matched her own shining black mane.

"Hey, Leesa," I said, after she calmed the jittery animal.

Leesa held out a card imprinted with a photo of her open, eager face. "I got it, Kath!"

"Congrats. So you'll be trading in Dynamite for the old Ford station wagon."

"I can't wait. This driver's license and that car are my tickets out of here."

I shook my head, never understanding why Leesa was so anxious to leave our small town. She always said "I want to see what's out there—not stay trapped in this boring place. There's nothing to do here anymore."

True, we couldn't go bowling because the lanes had closed down. Ditto for the movie theater and skating rink. Even back when everything was open, it was still six miles away—not an easy jaunt. And the nearest large town, Delores, was too far for anything but an occasional outing. But I gazed again at the far-away mountains, wearing white tops even in late May, and spread out my arms. "This is my home," I said. "I never want to leave."

"Still, you could get your driver's license." Leesa frowned. "But hell no, you had to be the only one in our whole class who didn't sign up for drivers ed."

"Then I'd have had to . . . our whole class? You mean all eight of us?" I laughed. "No cars for me. I might hurt Firefly's feelings."

"Everyone thinks you're weird."

"Especially Blanche?" I guessed.

Leesa giggled. "Especially Blanche."

Blanche Bennett had hated me since the day I entered Seguro Haven Elementary School and took Leesa away from her. "Lisa, that's my favorite name in the world," I'd said, astonishing her and myself. "You're going to be my new best friend." Leesa was so amazed by this greeting that she agreed at once. I didn't know Blanche had already staked a claim, and I hadn't meant to be cruel. But the name Lisa felt familiar and safe, and I desperately needed the familiar and safe. I didn't find out until much later that my new friend spelled her name differently.

Leesa had taught me how to drive, illegally, on remote mountain roads. So if the occasion ever arose—unlikely. I changed the subject. "So you'll be leaving next week?"

"Probably next Friday. Sure you won't come, too?"

"And destroy Blanche all over again? I don't think so. Besides, I'm needed at home."

This was true, but even if it wasn't, I had no interest in staying all summer at Blanche's sister's condo in Denver. Of course it was a great opportunity for Leesa—an apprentice position at the Denver Post, the first rung up the ladder in becoming a journalist.

Then I noticed her expression. I'd hurt her feelings; normally, she's pretty thick-skinned. "Maybe I could come for a visit," I said, knowing I'd never be allowed to. "I'll write you all the time."

Leesa nodded, and then gave a deep sigh. "Imagine me working on a newspaper . . . Oh, almost forgot. Mom wants to do a total makeover of my room while I'm away. You'll have to—"

"I'll take care of it," I said quickly. "Thanks." Leesa was referring to something she was hiding for me. She had that questioning look she gets when she wants to know more about my weird life. Not now, Leesa, I thought. Maybe not ever.

"It was a good year, wasn't it, Kath? Winning the apprenticeship, placing in swim team finals, the junior/senior prom . . ."

Things that didn't include me. Before Leesa could embark on a complete oral yearbook, I gave Firefly a let's-go pat. "Gotta go," I interrupted. "Lorelei may be home."

"Well, okay. See you later?"

"Firefly and I will ride over after supper to pick it up." Maybe Mark would have an idea for the next hiding place, I hoped.

August 25

Dear Kitty,

School started today, so of course it's the hottest day of the whole summer. To mark the occasion, I'm starting my fifth notebook of letters to you. I'm in high school now. A freshman at Carl Sandburg High, only a block away from where the poet lived. Not a very nice house. You have to make an appointment to go inside. Most people in town don't bother. They know it's there; they can go any time. I've visited, and I always say "Hi" when I walk by. I like his poetry because even though he experiments and takes risks, it makes sense to me. In fact, I like English—period. Maybe because there's not much to do at Aunt Kay's house other than read.

I wonder if you're in school, too. If you're still alive, you're sixteen—seventeen next March—so you're probably a junior. I can't imagine you any older than the last time I saw you. You looked kind of scary then, and you were mean to most people, but never to me.

My best friends are still Kevin and Brandon. Do you remember them? Your friend Lisa is Kevin's older sister.

Tim

P.S. What do you think Kevin and Brandon would say if they found out I've been keeping a diary (even if I call it a journal) for almost four years and that I'm writing to someone who's probably dead? You can blame my fifth-grade teacher for insisting we start diaries. "Diaries are for girls," the boys groaned, so the teacher said we should call them journals. I liked that but wasn't convinced until she said some people write pretend letters. That was better, especially when she said that even though we would write in them every school day, our journals were private. She would never read them. I think she hoped they'd become a habit with us. Well, in my case, she got her wish.

CHAPTER TWO

I'D HAVE KNOWN SHE WAS home, even if the brown van with its dirty windows and mud-caked license plates wasn't parked in back. Lights shone through all the downstairs windows. As I entered the front hall, I was overwhelmed by the smells of baking bread and roasting chicken.

When Lorelei was away, wispy, inefficient Mrs. Benway from town supposedly was in charge. Actually, we fended for ourselves, except at mealtimes. This trip must have gone well, I thought, for the house exuded joy and triumph. "Mother," I called out, and Lorelei rushed to greet me.

"I wish you still called me Mommy." She pouted briefly before flinging her arms around me.

I laughed and returned the hug. "Seventeen-year-olds don't say Mommy, silly." Most ten-year-olds don't either, although I did back then. In fact, I'd stopped using the childish name only a year ago.

Lorelei seemed flustered. "Seventeen already—are you sure?"

"Well, almost."

"That's right. June 8 is your homecoming day. Oh, dear, it won't be long before you'll be wanting to leave."

This time, I grabbed her. "No, this is my home. I never want to leave . . . Mommy."

She seemed to relax. "Guess what?"

"I already have. Because of the fancy meal you're fixing. Boy or girl?"

"Oh, Kathryn," Lorelei's tender eyes filled, "the most darling little girl. She's only seven, poor thing."

"Airport?"

"No, although I waited a long time in one. I found her outside a bus station—all by herself, running away—no parents and about to be placed in foster care." The tears flowed.

I handed Lorelei a tissue. "Well, she's home now," I said. "Have you named her yet?"

Lorelei shook her head. "I haven't had the chance. What do you think? You're better at names than I. It should begin with an A."

I played the naming game, as I had several times before. "Amy is cute," I said.

Lorelei frowned. I must have hit upon the real name, or something close. I tried again. "Anna?"

"Oh, lovely!" Lorelei clapped her hands. "Anna Harris is a lovely name."

"Shall I go introduce myself and bring her down to supper?"

Lorelei sighed. "No, Anna's homecoming feast will have to wait. She was so distraught I gave her something to help her sleep. You'll meet her tomorrow. Go pry your brother from his room. The rest of the children are watching cartoons in the kitchen."

I left before Lorelei could see my face redden. He's not my brother, I wanted to say, and all your pretending won't make it so.

Mark sat at his desk, his dark head bent over physics as he tried to make sense of the entire universe, since he couldn't comprehend our small one. I closed the door quietly behind me, just in case, and crept softly behind him. "Guess who?" I placed my hands over his eyes.

He whirled around suddenly, and I found myself on his lap with his lips on mine. I allowed some time to pass before I became indignant.

"Are you crazy?" I whispered, although I stayed where I was. "What if Lorelei comes in?"

"I'll say I'm giving you a brotherly greeting." Mark grinned. "If you're all that worried, why are you still here?"

I grinned back but got off. "It's time for supper."

"I know. The aroma of our mother's success preceded you." Mark stood and offered me his arm. "So, let us dine, but without the guest of honor, alas, for that fair lady has been drugged."

"Mark, no," I protested. "Anna was upset. Lorelei just gave her something to calm her down."

"Anna, is it? Well, believe what you want." He kissed me again. "This is getting really hard, Kath."

I nodded as we left the room and walked down the stairs.

The large oak table boasted Lorelei's best: a lace tablecloth, sterling silver, Waterford crystal, and Lennox china. Mark pecked Lorelei on the cheek. "This isn't supper, Mom. It's dinner for royalty."

Lorelei beamed. We joined hands while she said grace. "Lord, we thank you for this nourishing food. Please continue to bless the Harris family and help all children without love to find their way to us. And pay special heed to little Anna and guide her into adjusting to our ways. Amen."

"Amen," we all said. The children hesitated, worried about the unaccustomed grandness of the table. What might they accidentally break? And then what would happen?

"Now darlings," Lorelei said, "these dishes are to be used. I will not be angry if something is broken."

No, she never became angry with us, but her hurt and disappointment were harder to bear. My family! With the exception of Lorelei and Bobby, I had named each member and, including Bobby and possibly Lorelei, I did not know their real names. Although Mark was older, I had been here longer. He had been an angry, quarrelsome boy of thirteen when he arrived and I had given him his name. The younger children were Kyle (six) and Jenny (twelve). We pretended Bobby was fourteen, but he'd been that for as long as I'd known him, and he towered over the rest of us. Georgia should be thirteen by now, but I didn't want to think about her or David and Sarah, the two teenagers here when I first arrived. They left together after graduating high school almost six years ago—and never returned.

"How are you doing in school, Mark?" Lorelei asked, seemingly casual, although none of us were fooled.

Mark smiled pleasantly, but I sensed his inner rage. "Bs and Cs, as far as I know. I only have one final left before graduation."

"Excellent." Then she looked puzzled, the same look she'd given me earlier. "Graduation? Surely not yet."

"I'm eighteen, Lore . . . I mean, Mom."

"Oh, dear."

All parents, even pretend ones, must find it hard to accept their children growing up so fast. I hoped Lorelei wouldn't be unhappy when she found out about Mark's physics grade and the awards he was certain to get at graduation. It killed him to deliberately make mistakes to keep his grades down in his other subjects, but he did as Lorelei directed. He couldn't help shining in physics, though. Mark could easily have been class valedictorian. Okay, there were only ten in his class, but still . . .

The Harris children had been instructed never to do too well or too poorly in school (I got all Bs and Cs) and were not allowed to get into trouble. Harris children couldn't even go to school until Lorelei was certain they'd follow orders. We were always ill on picture-taking days. If we kept a low profile and weren't noticed—especially no newspaper photos—the Harris family would stay together. And of course that's what we all wanted—forever.

After dishes and making sure the children were occupied for the evening, Mark and I said goodnight to Lorelei, who always went to bed early when she was home, and saddled up Firefly and Mark's horse, Mr. Tom. "We won't be late, Mother. I promised Leesa we'd be over. She's leaving for Denver next week."

"Oh, yes . . ." Lorelei replied vaguely, "I suppose Leesa is growing up, too. Well, be good . . ."

Dear Kitty,

I'm enclosing this inside the journal. Why? Because it's important, and I want to keep it forever.

Tim

English 1, period 5
Mr. Robbins
Assignment: Personal biography
October 2

TIM'S STORY
by Timothy Allen Hunter

There's a lot to be said for Tim, whose name and body have been mine for over fourteen years. He's tall (approaching six feet) and has blond curly hair that he hates and girls want. He's well rounded—academics and swim team—and has a quirky sense of humor that gets him invited to parties. Yes, there's a lot to be said for Tim, but most people aren't interested. When they meet Tim for the first time, if they've lived in our town for a while, they always say "Aren't you the one—" I nod, but they continue anyway—"whose sister disappeared?"

Yeah, I'm the one, and it's probably the main reason I will leave Galesburg as soon as I graduate from Carl Sandburg High. I need a place where people have never heard of Katrina Hunter and would like to know her brother, Timothy.

When I was eight and my sister Kitty, ten, our father was killed in an accident. (Our mother died years before, and I have no memory of her; Kitty had only a trace.) The three of us had lived with my mother's older sister, Kay, who was cranky and hard to get along with but seemed to like me because I resembled my mother. After Dad died, Aunt Kay decided she couldn't be responsible for both of us and made arrangements for Kitty to travel to Boston, where some distant cousins of my father lived. She packed up Kitty, a briefcase containing important papers and a share of Dad's inheritance to give to the relatives for Kitty's "upbringing" and took her to O'Hare Airport in Chicago. She left Kitty alone for no more than fifteen minutes while she went to the washroom. But when she returned, Kitty, her bags, and the briefcase containing the money were gone. (Stupidly, Aunt Kay only believes in cash.)

The police searched, interviewed, and finally gave up. They had no leads. The airport is a busy place, and no one had seen anything they recalled. The newspapers, at least in Galesburg, hung in there longer. Every June 6, they observe the anniversary of her disappearance with a short article and a plea for information.

Through the years, I've lived alone with Aunt Kay, who decided it was actually Kitty she preferred after all. The Boston relatives stopped communicating. They blamed Aunt Kay, which was grossly unfair.

I don't blame anyone. I just wish I knew what happened. For a while, I thought I wanted to be a policeman when I grow up— or maybe a detective or an FBI agent. Then I decided on a newspaper reporter—maybe an investigative one like Woodward and Bernstein. I am grateful to the Galesburg Register for not giving up and for treating Aunt Kay and me with respect, unlike the TV reporters who kept asking us how we felt or making us feel like it was our fault.

Next year I'll be able to sign up for Journalism 1 and 2. I still want to be an investigative reporter and find out what happened to my sister and other people who disappear, but it's more than that now. I enjoy writing, and I want to be part of the newspaper world. I think telling people the truth is one of the most important things anyone can do.

A+

I would very much like to learn more about Timothy Hunter. Please consider joining the staff of the Sandburg High Gazette. We could use more writers like you.

Mr. Robbins, Gazette advisor.

CHAPTER THREE

THE HORSES TROTTED COMPANIONABLY ALONG the three-mile, semi-arid stretch that separated our home from the Dulows' ranch. Mark rode silently, although whether he was thinking about Lorelei, some complicated physics problem, or me, I couldn't tell.

"Mark," I said finally, "have you noticed how strange Lorelei acts whenever she realizes how old we are?"

"I was just thinking something like that. I know this sounds crazy, but maybe we should stop reminding her. And you might consider going back to calling her Mommy."

I nodded. If it weren't for Mark and me being together now, I'd wish he and I *were* kids again. It was easier to play Lorelei's family game then.

"Kathy, what do you remember about the older ones?" Mark sounded troubled. Why? And why was he asking about them now?

"David and Sarah? I don't remember much. They were here for such a short time after I came. They were nice to me, but we had about as much in common as you and I have with Kyle and Jenny."

"They just disappeared?"

"Sort of. I think maybe Lorelei sent them away. They had a horrible fight with her." I had heard their angry voices as I lay in my bed upstairs. I couldn't tell what they were saying.

"I don't want to be sent away," Mark said.

"Me, neither."

Firefly whinnied with delight as we rode through the entrance of Hidden Jewel Ranch. "Yes, you did it, old girl. Thank you, Firefly," I told the sensitive mare. "You'll get a fine treat here."

The Hidden Jewel, for which the ranch was named, was a silver mine discovered by Leesa's great-grandfather. Abandoned for years, the mine had made Great Grandpa Dulow and his heirs wealthy, and they used their money for the jewels that mattered most to them—horses.

Donna Dulow, Leesa's mother, was coming out of the stables as we approached. The tools she carried meant she'd been mucking out the stalls, but she still managed to look as neat as if she were going to a fancy restaurant in Durango. She resembled a slightly older version of her eldest daughter.

"Hey, Donna, taking over the stable boy's job?"

Donna laughed. "Not really, Kathryn, but I have a skittish mare who doesn't calm down for anyone but me. Leesa is in the house. She told me Lorelei has returned."

"This afternoon. She's adopted a little girl."

"That woman's an absolute saint." Donna sighed. "So many children throughout the years. And all of you turned out well. Yes, even you, Mark, although you were a rascal when you first came. Have you heard anything from David and Sarah? Best workers I ever had."

I looked pleadingly at Mark, not really in the mood to play Lorelei's game of *What if someone asks you about________________, what will you say?*

Almost by rote, Mark gave the agreed-upon answer to the question. "David is married. He and his wife live in Hawaii. Sarah just finished grad school somewhere in upstate New York. They write occasionally, and Lorelei goes to see them."

Donna smiled. "I suppose they are too busy to pay us a visit. Next time you write, give them my best. Have you heard from our Miss Personality?"

Mark turned away. I'd have to answer. "No, but Lorelei didn't think we would. Georgia is with her aunt and uncle now, living a new life. But we all miss her."

"I don't know if I could have been as brave as Lorelei and let her go. But as I said, she is a saint. I've often wondered what it's like being a part of the Harris family."

For one thing, you have to be a really good liar, I thought. Mark and I said goodbye and hurried into the house.

We found Leesa in her room, which resembled a hotel suite more than a regular bedroom. She handed me a locked briefcase. Even though she must have been curious, I was positive she had never tried to open the cheap lock—never tried to take so much as a peek inside. Leesa was honest. I was ashamed suddenly of all the secrets. I didn't deserve such a friend. Impulsively, I gave her a hug.

Giggling, Leesa hugged back. "What was that for? We're not saying goodbye yet, and even then it's only for the summer."

"Just thanks for being you," I said.

"We'd better get back," Mark said gruffly. "Lorelei may need our help with Anna."

Actually, we need to find a place to hide the briefcase, I said silently.

Leesa squealed. "A new sister? How wonderful! Is she a baby?"

We told Leesa what little we could about Anna, then made our escape before she could talk us into staying longer.

Mark held the briefcase until I mounted Firefly. Fortunately, I'd have no trouble riding with only one hand free. I'd trust Firefly even if I had no hands. For a few seconds my eyes smarted as the feel and smell of the briefcase brought my father back to me. No! No room in this life for past emotions!

I hadn't opened it in close to a year—not since last summer when I'd needed money to help Georgia. Almost seven years ago, I'd emptied it, replacing the contents with drawings that had been in my suitcase. After proudly showing Lorelei my pictures, I'd returned the money. I'd never kept it in one place too long—the back of my closet, the attic, Firefly's stall. Once I'd even stuffed some of the money into my desk at school. Leesa had been the briefcase's keeper since Georgia left.

Once Hidden Jewel was behind us, Mark interrupted my thoughts. "What's in it, Kath? Identification papers?"

I nodded. "Yes, and a few letters and a lot of money. I used to hide it at home. I suppose I could again, but—"

Mark snorted. "I suppose you couldn't. I have an idea, though."

He led me off the trail and into Juniper Forest. I realized then that Mark was thinking about more than where to put the briefcase.

"Whoa," Mark instructed both horses as we were about to pass a thick grove of junipers that had an opening no one knew about but us—I hoped. "Care to stop here for a while, Kathy?"

I blushed furiously while the rest of my body responded with a longing I'd scarcely known about until a few months before. The grove was where Mark and I first made love. Back in March we were still trying to ignore our feelings, pretending to be just friends, for we had never thought of ourselves as brother and sister. Lorelei was off pursuing orphans, and Mark and I decided to go camping, even though it was still plenty cold. We each had our own sleeping bag, but I couldn't sleep. I'd just finished reading Hemingway's *For Whom the Bell Tolls* for an English book report; Mark read it last year. Alone in my bag, I couldn't help thinking about Robert Jordan and Maria, sharing the one bag. Later, Mark said he'd remembered that part of the book, too.

Mark was waiting for an answer. "I do want to stop—for a long while," I admitted. "But what about the briefcase?"

Mark looked at me intently. "But we'll come back soon?"

"Soon," I promised. We leaned toward each other and kissed, until Mr. Tom let us know he was tired of being so chummy with Firefly.

We rode on until we came to a wreck of a hunter's shack. I'd played there a few times after I first came to Seguro Haven. Then a boy received a severe puncture wound from a rusty nail and *Keep Out* signs were posted.

We kids moved on to new haunts. No one had ever bothered to take down the shack, though.

"Are you sure this is a safe place? Kids might still play here, even though Kyle and Jenny aren't allowed to."

Mark shrugged. "Doesn't look like anyone has been here for years, but fire is probably a greater danger than kids fooling around. We won't hide it inside. There are a lot of hollow trees around. I've got some plastic bags in my saddlebag. We'll divide your loot and stash it inside different trees."

It wasn't a great idea, but I didn't have a better one. We dismounted and tied the horses to two posts next to the shack. "Let's separate and look for the right trees," Mark said. "The hollows can't be so deep we won't be able to reach the bags again."

"Or so obvious some child may find them," I added.

We spread out, and I found some possible hiding places. I guessed Mark had, too, for he called out to me. His voice sounded funny, though. Not like him.

I rushed to where I'd heard him. Mark, sickly pale, gestured into a thick grove of aspens. "What's wrong?"

"Come." Warning me not to touch the sagebrush loaded with ticks this time of year, Mark led me into the grove, and then pointed to the ground. "There," he said, voice shaking.

There, side-by-side, I saw two longish mounds of dirt. "So?"

"Don't you think they look like graves?"

"Well, maybe a little. But I don't know what could be buried that's shaped like that, except… maybe… *people?*"

Mark bent down and using his hand as a shovel, tentatively began to dig next to the longest mound.

I yanked him away. "Mark, you are not going to dig up whatever's there. It's probably nothing anyway, and we have to hide my papers and money. I think it might be better if everything stayed together in the locked briefcase."

Mark stood, and as he did, I saw a flash of gold on the ground. In wonder, I picked up the object. A boy's class ring. "Oh, no," I whispered, knowing what would be engraved inside even before I wiped away the dirt. Before I could stop them, disturbing voices crashed into my head, forcing me to remember.

Everyone else will have a ring. Sarah and I want one, too.

Well, you wouldn't give us the money, so we went to the ranch and earned it on our own.

When? When you were out stalking Kathy, of course.

No, we won't give them to you, and you know what we'll do if you make us.

"What is it, Kath?" I handed Mark the ring, and we looked at the engraving together: S.H.H.S. Class of 1999, D.H. "Let's get out of here," Mark said quietly, putting the ring into his pocket.

Without speaking, without consulting each other, we returned to our grove. We got off the horses and collapsed into each other's arms—this time for comfort. "We don't know it was them," I whispered into his ear.

"A mighty good guess, though," Mark said grimly. "Happy graduation, David and Sarah."

"But who do you think?" I stopped. If Mark hadn't been holding me, I would have fallen. "Mark, no. Not Lorelei!"

Suddenly I heard a rustling in the bushes. Someone was watching us, although I didn't think anyone could have heard our conversation. I broke away from Mark and ran toward the noise. Better to know what the danger was. Galloping away was a cream-colored mare I recognized, and on her back sat someone with fiery red hair. "Blanche Bennett," I said, when Mark joined me. "It was Blanche Bennett, who absolutely despises me."

October 12

Dear Kitty,

Good times! My team took a first at the swim meet. Best friends Kevin and Brandon are also on the team, and I would stick with it even if we lost every time. When I swim, I am released, and my thoughts flow freely along with my body. No matter what kind of foul mood I'm in (trust me, I can get plenty moody), swimming cheers me right up. Do you have any sport that makes you feel that way?

I see your old friend Lisa sometimes. She's very, very popular and has a steady boyfriend, a big football star, believe it or not. She's just an average student, but I don't think she cares. When we pass each other in the hall, she always says "Hi," even if she's with her friends. I don't think she ever forgot you. I haven't either.

Your brother,
Tim

P.S. Guess what? It's definite! I'm doing so well in English class I'll be allowed to join the newspaper staff, even though I'm only a freshman!

CHAPTER FOUR

BEFORE GOING HOME, WE RETURNED to the ranch and told Leesa what Blanche had seen—well, we sort of told her. "I hurt my arm and Mark was comforting me," I said, "but Blanche will think it's something else."

Leesa frowned. "I'll make Blanche promise not to say anything," she said, "but I wish you'd tell me the truth. Anyone with eyes can see how it is with you two. It's not like you're actually related."

It was the only time I'd ever seen Mark blush. He turned away. "Lorelei wouldn't understand," I said. "Please talk to Blanche."

Although not quite ten, the house was dark. "Everyone's asleep," I said. "That's good." Then I remembered. "We forgot to hide the briefcase."

"You're right, but I still don't think it's safe to take it inside." Mark paused a moment. "Hand it over, and I'll go find someplace, even if it's only temporary. My hollow tree idea was lousy."

I gripped Firefly's reins so tightly my hands hurt. "But you have it, don't you?"

A long silence. "No."

"Where did we leave it?" I whispered, afraid that a normal volume would make the words real. Mark didn't bother answering. There were three possibilities: Leesa's house, the dirt mounds, or Juniper Grove. "What shall we do?"

"I'll go back and search. You get Firefly settled and go inside. If Lorelei wakes up, she'll be less suspicious if only one of us is gone. Besides, you can tell her something."

"Like what?"

Mark scowled. "Invent something. Do what we always do—lie." First grabbing a lantern from the back porch, he and Mr. Tom set out again.

I led Firefly into the barn, stroking her and saying soothing words that were really meant for me. "Mr. Tom will be back soon. It will be okay. He and Mark will find it. Lorelei won't wake up—she never does."

"Kathy talks to horses . . . Kathy talks to horses," sing-songed a voice that wasn't quite a child's or yet a man's.

I shrieked loudly enough to awaken all of Seguro Haven before I recognized—Bobby! "Bobby, you scared me to death! What are you doing here so late?"

"I'm listening to you talk to horses," Bobby said, sounding smug. "Kathy talks to horses—"

"Of course I do. Everyone does." Then I noticed what he was holding. "Bobby, what *are* you doing?"

"I wanted to say goodnight to Mama Cat and her babies."

"With a shovel?"

Bobby gave the shovel a confused look before hanging it back on the wall where it belonged. "It was on the ground. I picked it up."

Bobby was lying. He was the only one of us who wasn't any good at it, which was one of the many reasons he stayed at home. He was, as they say, mentally challenged and was home-schooled by Mrs. Benway and the rest of us when we had time or thought about it. Lorelei always said he'd be too noticeable in a public school.

But Bobby was big and strong and had been carrying a heavy shovel. I shuddered, forcing the crazy, scary thoughts away. I would ignore his lie— for now. It was late and also possible that someone else had heard me screech. "You help me put Firefly to bed, and then I'll tuck you into yours," I said, knowing that both were among Bobby's favorite things.

"Okay," he agreed eagerly. Then "Where's Mark? What do Mr. Tom and Mark want to find?"

He'd heard. Well, I might need a cover story for Lorelei anyway. I thought fast. "Mark thought he heard a wildcat. He's just checking. He'll be back soon."

"Bobby will wait for him," he declared.

I groaned. "Oh, no, he won't. Just look at Firefly. She's so tired she's falling asleep standing up."

Bobby giggled. "That's the way horses sleep, Kathy." But he helped me unfasten the saddle, giving up the notion of waiting for Mark. That job would fall upon me.

My heart pounding, I lay awake for hours, it seemed, waiting to hear footsteps outside my door—Mark's or Lorelei's. I considered the weak cover story I'd told Bobby and hoped I wouldn't have to use it again—and I hoped Bobby wouldn't repeat it. Bobby's memory was limited, though, and he'd been more impressed with his little joke about sleeping horses than he'd been with Mark's whereabouts.

Bobby's shovel story bothered me. Why had it been on the ground? Bobby was lying, but what was the truth? Unless it was to feed Nelly and see her kittens, Mark and I were normally the only ones who went into the barn. Lorelei was afraid of horses, and our two—Firefly and Mr. Tom—actually belonged to Leesa's family. Bobby and Mark were the only ones tall enough to reach the shovel when it was stored properly; even I was taller than Lorelei now. Probably Bobby had taken it down himself and then felt guilty. But I was troubled by the proximity of shovels and dug graves.

Oh, where was Mark? I wondered if Leesa had called Blanche, or if she was waiting to see her at school. Not for the first time I wished I hadn't made an enemy of Blanche. It wasn't just claiming Leesa as my best friend so many years ago. Because of my unwillingness to share, I'd never treated Blanche like she even existed, or at least anyone to be taken seriously—until now, when it might be too late.

What would Lorelei do if she found out about Mark and me? Was I afraid of her? Ridiculous, for no one loved me more than she. And after Mark and a little boy who appeared occasionally in my dreams, I loved her best, too.

What's wrong, darling? Why are you crying?

No one picks me, Mommy. They say I can't catch.

I'll teach you, dear. We'll practice and practice until everyone wants you on their team.

I can't sleep, Mommy. I had a nightmare.

Then I'll hold you, my darling, until you fall asleep again.

Lorelei. I'd only started using that name last summer when her mistake with Georgia made me question and grow fearful. Before that, I'd stuck with "Mommy," as juvenile as it sounded. No, Lorelei would never do anything really wrong. The dirt mounds couldn't possibly conceal bodies. There must be a rational explanation as to why David's ring was there. He could have dropped it, or maybe someone stole it. I tried to take comfort from explanations that were not logical.

My door opened slowly, and then closed again. "Who's there?" I whispered.

"It's me, Kath. Move over."

I made room in my bed but said "This is not a good idea, and it's really late."

"I'm cold, and I want to hold you. Just for a few minutes. Let me tell you what happened, then I'll leave."

"Okay, but if anyone comes, get under the covers."

Mark had found the briefcase at the first place he'd looked, Juniper Grove. "Where is it now?" I whispered.

"Hidden Jewel Mine. No one goes there anymore. It's inside the entrance in back of rusty tools and old sacks."

I sighed. "I wish you'd thought of the mine in the first place." For if he had, we never would have seen the mounds, and Blanche Bennett would not have seen us. "You should go." Before you get too cozy, I added silently. "School tomorrow. Exams for both of us."

"It's probably tomorrow already." Mark paused, still not leaving. "Kath, I've done something stupid—maybe even dangerous."

I waited.

"I lied about my grades this semester. I'm getting straight A's, and I took the SATs and ACTs and Advanced Placement Tests for college. I got top scores. My history teacher had me apply for scholarships to a few colleges and thinks I'll be offered something. And I'm afraid I'm going to be valedictorian, even though my grades for the other years were only a little above average. They're still better than everyone else's."

"Mark!"

He scrambled under the covers. "Shhhh!" he hissed.

"Why, Mark?" I whispered as soon as I thought it was safe.

"Because I want to be like other kids. I want to go to college and come home *here* for vacations. What does Lorelei expect me to do next year?"

"I don't know." Lorelei never talked about our futures; she never mentioned what we would do when we grew up. In some ways, I wanted to be a regular kid, too. It would be nice not to have to lie, for instance. I didn't want to go to college, though. I'd rather stay here and maybe work for the Dulows training horses. But I understood how Mark felt. "Go to bed, dear," I said. "Try not to worry. We'll think of something."

Much later, long after Mark left, I heard sobbing in the room next to mine. It was the new girl, Anna. "Mama!" she cried out. "Please take me home to my mama!"

November 4

Dear Kitty,

Election Day, and I covered it for Sandburg High Gazette. Did you just say "So what? High schoolers can't vote?" Well, excuse me! We're very serious about voting at our school, and I was excited to be allowed to write an article that will be published in both our paper and the town's. One of the reasons was that I was willing to get up early and walk along with the dozen seniors who had turned eighteen.

We met outside the school and marched all the way to City Hall. Some carried placards, and some were having deep discussions that verged on arguments. Everyone was peaceful, though. Mainly it was just a proud time, and I was proud being a part of it.

I interviewed them about how it felt to be eighteen and voting and asked them what candidates they supported and why. They treated me with respect, even though I'm four years younger. Maybe they just wanted to make sure I spelled their names right, if they actually ended up in the paper.

Mr. Robbins made a few corrections but was complimentary. The article will be published under my byline. I wish I could show it to you. Heck, I wish Aunt Kay would read it and be impressed!

Tim

I USED MY FINGERS TO comb out my bleached hair. The brown roots were becoming too apparent. Time for a dye job—and a haircut. Abandoning my natural comb, I grabbed a hairbrush and swooped my untidy mane into a ponytail. No matter; soon it would be summer vacation, and I'd hardly see anyone, so the blond disguise wouldn't matter as much. My eyes would, though. Groaning with anticipated pain, I inserted the brown contacts over my blue eyes. Cheap vanity things, but the best Lorelei could do without a doctor's prescription. Harris kids didn't see doctors. Lorelei paid cash for basic shots at the local drugstore. What would she do if any of them got really sick? Well, we couldn't—that's all!

Gosh, I was tired. Good thing my grades on finals weren't important. Mark's were to him, though. I wondered how he was feeling this morning.

Next door I heard voices—Lorelei soothing Anna. Over and over Lorelei was chanting "Your name is Anna, and you're my little girl now. Your name is Anna, and I am your mommy." Lorelei's brainwashing was always effective. Soon Anna would be one of us.

Brainwashing? Had I really thought that word? Lorelei's way of welcoming strangers was loving and nurturing. She was behaving the same as always. The change must be in me.

Mark glowered over his cereal as the other children chattered happily. "It will be so much fun," Jenny said. "Right after school, we're going to Hidden Jewel Ranch for the whole weekend."

"Lorelei left a note," Mark muttered.

"Can I go too?" Kyle asked.

"Yes," Jenny said. "And Kathy and Mark and—"

"Me, too!" Bobby shouted.

"Well, I don't know." Jenny looked troubled. "It's not like you go to school."

"I'm sure the invitation includes Bobby," I said, not really knowing but always acting as peacemaker. "We'll have a start-of-summer celebration."

But Mark and I exchanged a long glance of perfect understanding. They were being sent away so that Lorelei would have the weekend alone with Anna, that poor little girl. Something was different and wrong. Or maybe I was just finally noticing.

"Let's go, gang," Mark said suddenly. "Time and tide and school bus wait for no man."

Giggling, the children grabbed their bags and followed Mark. Bobby seemed dejected. "Cheer up, Bobby," I said, lagging behind. "Mrs. Benway will be here soon, and I'm sure you're coming to the ranch with us."

"That's because Mommy loves Anna best now. She always loves new people best."

I sighed, hoping I wouldn't miss the bus, but Bobby's feelings were important. "That's not true, Bobby. Mommy loves all of us best. She just wants to help Anna feel at home. She doesn't want Anna to have to meet so many new people at once."

"Anna is sad," Bobby said. "Anna wants her real mommy."

"Anna's real mommy is dead, Bobby. That's why she came here. She's an orphan now."

"That's not what Anna said. And how come she has to change her name if she's an orphan?"

Wow! Every now and then Bobby showed a glimmer of intelligence. He had a point. Runaways were different, but why would anyone have to change names if they weren't hiding? And why hadn't I ever thought about it before? "Yikes! I've got to get the bus, Bobby." I stretched on tiptoes to plant a kiss on his forehead. "You be good now!"

Mark had saved a seat for me. "That was close," he said, as the bus pulled out.

I shrugged. "Bobby was upset, and Mrs. Benway is late. Mark, you look worse than I feel."

"No sleep does that. This weekend, Kath, we've got to find time together." At my look, he said quickly, "Not necessarily for that, although it would be a bonus. Things are happening fast, and we need to plan."

I wasn't sure what he meant but nodded anyway. Even if everything else was okay, Mark wasn't.

"And Kath, I think you should bring your key along. I'd like to examine those papers of yours, and maybe you'd be willing to give me some money, just in case."

Mark was thinking of leaving, I thought, wondering how to change his mind, but we couldn't discuss it on the school bus. "Well, here we are" was the next thing I said. "Good luck on finals, Mark."

He smiled. "By noon I'll be done. See you later."

History ended at noon. I probably failed, but it didn't matter. Maybe I'd drop out next year and stay home and help Bobby. No, Lorelei wouldn't allow that. Calling the school's attention to our family was to be avoided at all costs. For the first time I wondered how she had enrolled us. Didn't you need birth certificates? That was why Mark and I couldn't get our drivers licenses. He was right that we should examine the papers in the briefcase—something I'd never done, mainly because I didn't want to know. I was happy here and didn't want anything to change. Never question, I had been told often. This is your life now.

Your name is Kathryn. Your name is Kathryn Harris. Some people call you Kathy. That's all right. They may call you Kath, too. Never anything else. Do you hear me? Your name is Kathryn, Kathy, Kath, and you are my daughter now. You will call me Mommy.

Brainwashing. Just like Anna. Kind and loving, but brainwashing, none-the-less. That was why I never questioned. But my name was Kitty, even though I didn't like the name or want to remember.

I had one more exam after lunch—Home Economics. I would do well; I certainly had had enough experience. I looked up and down the hall for Mark. We didn't have a plan exactly, but he should have waited. I checked the student message board. Nothing for me.

Mark wasn't in the cafeteria, but Leesa was, sitting next to Blanche. She waved me over. Reluctantly, I joined them.

"One more to go," I said cheerily.

"You look like hell," Leesa said. "Rough night?"

Blanche snorted, but I ignored her. "House was hot. I couldn't get comfortable." I changed the subject. "Seems we're spending the weekend at the ranch. You coming, too, Blanche?" Might as well be friendly.

She shook her head. "No, I've got to get ready for Denver. Too bad you can't go with us. I guess you can't leave a certain someone."

I laughed, pretending not to know what she meant. "I can't leave a lot of someones. My mother needs help with the children, but I'm going to see if I can get a job with Leesa's parents."

Leesa shot Blanche a warning glance before saying "I'm sure they'd be glad to have you. You can ask tonight."

Aw, the heck with Blanche, I needed to know. "Have either of you seen Mark? I thought he'd wait for me after his last final."

Blanche couldn't resist. "Just can't stay away from him, can you? Too, too sweet."

Leesa slammed down her tray, causing the dishes to wobble precariously. "That's it! Blanche, you're my friend, but so is Kathy. If you can't knock off the snotty remarks, I'll find another place to stay in Denver. My parents wouldn't mind. If you can't be decent to Kathy, I don't want to stay with you."

Both Blanche and I stared at Leesa. It took a lot to get her steamed up. "I'm sorry," Blanche said. "I was only teasing." Her face turned as red as her hair.

"That's okay," I said, "but I'd rather you didn't. Mark and I are together, but we aren't related. Our guardian wouldn't understand, though."

"So it's nothing to joke about," Leesa said firmly. "I saw Mark going into the office, Kath. He said there was a message for him. I don't know anything more, but I'm sure we'll catch up with him at the ranch later."

Later it would have to be, whether I liked it or not. Time now to cook a breakfast that would earn a modest grade in Home Ec.

The children and I met a proud Leesa in the parking lot—first time driving to school with her new license. She suggested we go straight to the ranch without bothering to go home first. Kyle and Jenny, exuberant to be done with school, cheered loudly, too loud for me to be heard until they were done.

"Okay, settle down, children," I said. "Leesa, go ahead and take these silly goofuses. I need to check in with Mark and Lorelei. Could you drop me off and pick up Bobby? I'll ride out later with Mark. We'll want the horses this weekend, anyway, and we'll pack clothing for everyone."

"Well, okay . . . But, Bobby . . ." Leesa wasn't thrilled with the plan, but she'd go along with it. "Well, okay, but don't you think these kids are getting mighty old to be called children?"

Jenny and Kyle beamed in agreement. I hadn't realized they felt that way. "You're right," I said. "It's time they graduated. It's just that's what Lorelei always calls them . . ." And what she called Mark and me, too.

Mark and Lorelei weren't home, and Mrs. Benway had no idea where they were.

"Are they together?" I asked. Mrs. Benway didn't think so. Mrs. Harris had left that morning on "business."

Business? It was too soon to bring back another child, which seemed to be Lorelei's only business. "Business?"

"Monkey business, if you ask me."

Mrs. Benway was normally grumpy, but this seemed different. Instinct said I needed to find out what was wrong.

"Kathy? Yippee! Can I go to the ranch now? I'm all packed!" As usual, Bobby interrupted at the worst possible time. Well, maybe not. It might help if I disposed of him before talking further with the unhappy housekeeper.

"Everyone is waiting for you in Leesa's car, Bobby. I'll take you there right now." I turned to Mrs. Benway. "Then I'd like to talk more with you."

"I'd best see to Anna," she said. "The child has the sniffles."

I walked Bobby down the long, narrow driveway. Cars rarely drove all the way up to the house. Turning around was tricky, especially for an inexperienced driver.

"Does Anna have a cold? Maybe Mommy went to buy her some medicine."

"Nope. She's crying. She's been crying all day long. She wants her mommy."

"Bobby, we've talked about this. Anna is sad because her real mommy died."

Bobby shook his head. "I don't think so."

Could Bobby be right? Lorelei said Anna was an orphan. If so, Lorelei had lied. Well, what would be so surprising about that? All of them lied—that's what they'd been taught to do. But not about something like this. Claiming that a child was an orphan when she wasn't . . . That was kidnapping! Maybe Lorelei had made another mistake, like with Georgia.

Bobby scrambled into the front seat, taking my place. He so rarely had the chance to be away from home and while his behavior wasn't always appropriate, he was friendly and adored being with other children. Children. That word again. I wondered how old Bobby was. Older than Mark, I imagined. Not even a minor.

Leesa glanced at Bobby. "Are you sure you won't come?" I shook my head. "Mark home yet?" Again, I shook my head. "We need to talk, Kath. Soon." I nodded before turning back to the house. Something was troubling Leesa—maybe something about Bobby? I shrugged. It was a short car ride. No time to worry about it now.

Mrs. Benway was puttering aimlessly in the kitchen, distracted even for her.

"How's Anna," I asked. She shrugged. "I'm surprised Lorelei left Anna so soon. Are you sure you don't know where she is?"

"Probably harassing William again," she muttered.

"William? You mean your husband—Mr. Benway?"

She turned to me, furious. I had never seen her in such a state. "Only William I know. I finally threw the pathetic coward out. Can't even stand up to his baby sister. I won't be a party to it any longer. Children coming and going like stray cats, and I'm supposed to shut up and not notice."

I sat down, suddenly dizzy. "His sister? You don't mean—Lorelei?" I squeaked her name.

She scoffed. "Josephine. Josephine Grace Benway. No, that wasn't fancy enough. I don't know where she got this Lorelei nonsense. So she's had a hard life. Who hasn't? That doesn't give her the right to mess in other people's and to blackmail her brother."

"Blackmail?"

"Well, maybe not. But for sure he's done things he shouldn't be proud of." She turned her back on me. "I need to get back to my work. No more foolish questions."

"Only a few of us here for dinner tonight, Mrs. Benway. Why don't you go home? I'll tell Lorelei it was okay. Let me take care of Anna."

"Well, I will. I might even be gone forever. My sister wants me now that she's alone. Suddenly, I'm good enough company." She took off her apron and hung it on a hook. "There's some TV dinners in the freezer you can fix. As for the little girl, you can do as much as I could. She's in there crying her heart out, and the door is locked."

November 22

Dear Kitty,

Happy Thanksgiving. I hope you're having a good one. Brandon and I cheered on the home team, even though we lost against Kewanee. Sandburg High has a much better team, but our players were just phoning it in today. No enthusiasm whatsoever. I whipped up an article about the game, which I'll revise later. Gotta keep it positive. I don't need big, mean football players angry with me.

Brandon's family invited Aunt Kay and me over for dinner. He has a large, friendly family, and I was determined to go. We'd be lucky to have frozen TV dinners here. Aunt Kay balked, but I talked her into it. She can be pleasant when she gets outside of her own head. So I said that I was going and that if she didn't, everyone would talk about her. That did the trick! Not easy, but sometimes you just gotta put your foot down.

Gobble! Gobble! Hope it's great!

Tim

CHAPTER SIX

THE PHONE RANG AS I started upstairs. The only one in the house was in the living room. Leesa always bemoaned the fact I didn't own a cell. None of us did, not even Lorelei. It was probably her on a pay phone; there were still some around. "Hello . . ."

"Hey, Kath. Leesa. Wanted you to know that Mark just got here—on Mr. Tom, so you won't need to wait for him."

"Thanks."

"So you'll be here soon? You sound funny."

"Yeah, I'll be there later, but I've got to go now. See ya . . ."

"Oh, okay . . . But Kathy, Blanche just called. She said she saw Mrs. Harris at the drugstore. Blanche almost didn't recognize her because she was wearing a blond wig."

In town? Lorelei needed to be more careful. "Mistaken identity," I said. "Look, Leesa, I've really got to go—like to the bathroom. See ya soon."

At some point, I needed to decide about Leesa. She had always been such a good friend to me, while I—No time to think about it. First, Anna.

I knew where the key was because of the time I helped Georgia. I had found it in Lorelei's jewelry box, covered by junk jewelry she never wore. Georgia was different from the rest of us, twelve then, but somehow more mature and less willing to fit in. Lorelei had locked her in the Starting Room after Georgia mouthed off too many times, and then left on one of her mysterious errands. Georgia had started pounding on the door, yelling so loud I decided to find the key. It wasn't difficult.

Look, this is a huge mistake. I'm not an orphan. Had a big fight with my mom and was fooling around with the idea of running away. I was sitting on a bench outside the depot when Mrs. Harris came along.

"But, Georgia, you went with her," I'd said.

I guess I must have. I remember that she took me inside and got me something to drink. We talked a little, but that's all I remember. Then I was here, and everyone, including you, said my name was Georgia and that Mrs. Harris was my mother. I got so confused.

You're saying you're not an orphan—that your parents are still alive?

I live with my mom—it's just the two of us. She didn't want me to go to this party because the parents were out of town and—Oh, she was right. I was being a brat, but I didn't see it that way then.

And you want to go home. Do you remember where it is?

Yes. Can you help me? Your mom might be nice, even though she isn't to me, but my name is Genevieve—VeeVee for short—and I want to go home.

I gave Georgia some money, and she walked away—probably the whole six miles into town. I never saw her again. Had Lorelei made another "mistake?" I couldn't just give Anna money and send her on her way. She was seven.

I retrieved the key, grateful it was in the same place. The room hadn't changed since I'd been there last—as neat as if it had passed an army inspection. Bed neatly made, covered with a plain white spread, framed prints of mountains that might have come from a calendar—the room was cold, sterile, devoid of personality.

I walked down the long hall and unlocked the Starting Room door. I was shocked by Anna's appearance—face mottled red and white, eyes puffy slits. I rushed to her bed, but she stayed stiff in my arms and would not be comforted.

"It's all right, Anna. It's all right."

She flung herself away from me. "No! I'm not Anna. I'm Amy, and I want to go home!" Her tears started again. "Please help me?"

Could I tell Lorelei she'd made a mistake? No, I could not. "I will help you, Amy, but we must be very careful. I need you to trust me." Not that there was any reason she should. "Try to tell me what you remember. How did you happen to come here?"

Through gulps, sobs, and sniffles, the story came together. Amy and her mother had been in a large department store buying shoes when Amy wandered away. "I didn't mean to, but waiting for Mama was boring. She couldn't decide which shoes to buy." I patted her hand, encouraging her to continue. "The store was too big, and I got lost. I couldn't find my way back. I was going to ask a salesperson to help me, but this lady came and said she would. She said she knew a shortcut to the shoe department."

"Lorelei," I said. "The person who told you your name was Anna." Even though I had named her. That part was my fault.

"She said she's my mama, but she's not!"

"I know she isn't. Go on."

"I forget the rest. I went to sleep, I think. Then I woke up in a dark van, and then I came here."

This wasn't about helping orphans and abused children any longer. Lorelei, what happened to you? Or have you always been like this, but I loved you too much to notice? Or I needed to love you, to believe you were good, or I would have been the one to blame—the one who made the mistake.

"I promise that you will go home," I said, "but I need to figure out how. Let's get you washed up, but then I'm afraid I'm going to have to lock you in again until I come up with a plan." She looked at me, eyes terrified, and I remembered.

I want to tell Aunt Kay I didn't mean to. I'll go to Boston. If I behave better, maybe I can go home and see Tim again. I miss him, and he'll be so sad without me.

That's when Lorelei locked me in.

Mommy, please unlock the door. I'll be Kathryn, I promise. I don't like being locked in. Please let me out. I'll be good again.

That was me back then. And I was ten, not seven. Then I met David, Sarah, and Bobby. I fell in love with the horses, the land, and the mountains. Then I met Leesa and Mark came.

"No, Amy. I will not lock you in again." I took her into the bathroom and dropped the key down the drain. Maybe Lorelei would forget she locked the door. The thing to do was pretend everything was okay. Lorelei had always confused easily. Lately, even more so than usual.

Amy and I were having lemonade and peanut butter cookies in the kitchen when the phone rang again. "Don't worry," I said. "I'll be right back." Would it be Mark, Leesa, or Lorelei?

"Oh, Kathryn dear, it's Mommy. I need to speak with Mrs. Benway. Get her for me, please."

A lie. Quick! "She just went down to the mailbox, Mommy." The mailbox was quite a distance from the house. Hopefully, that would work. "Everything is fine here. I can take a message."

"Well . . . maybe you can." Briefly, Lorelei said that she would not return home that night or maybe not for a few. "I'm concerned about Anna."

"Oh, don't be, Mommy. Anna is fine, and she is adorable. She and I have been eating a snack in the kitchen, and I've been telling her all about us. She's even been laughing. I'm going to show her the kittens and promised her that as soon as they're old enough to leave their mother, she may have one to keep. She is so excited."

"She is? She's happy now?" I had never heard Lorelei so flustered. I wondered if she was thinking of a certain key and a locked room.

"Yes, she's seems perfectly adjusted. Shall I call her to the phone?"

"No, that's all right," Lorelei said quickly. "Do you think we should consider a new brother or sister then? A boy would be nice."

Oh, no! "Maybe not yet, Mommy. We're all a bit jealous and would like to have you to ourselves for a while. Mark was saying this morning how much he misses you."

"Mark did?"

I laughed. That was far-fetched. "Well, he did say that we eat a whole lot better when you're home. Mrs. Benway's meals . . . well, you know. That's Mark's way of saying he misses you."

Then Lorelei laughed, too, although it didn't sound natural to me. "Where are the children? I thought you were going to the ranch."

"They're all there. I needed to come home and get something first. I'll go as soon as Mrs. Benway returns with the mail." I needed to end this, so I called out "I'm coming, Anna!" I chuckled. "She is so anxious to see the kittens."

"I'll let you go then. Tell Mrs. Benway I should return late tomorrow. I'll see you Sunday or Monday."

"Bye, Mommy. I love you." The darned thing about that, of course, was I meant it.

Before returning to the kitchen, I thought of something—Mrs. Benway saying that Lorelei's name was really Josephine. Usually, we stuck to the same initial. Why did Lorelei pick that name? Did it mean anything? If I were at school or the ranch, I could have looked it up on the Internet, but computers didn't exist in the Harris household. I took the dictionary from the bookshelf and found it quickly. Of German origin, I read. "Legends say that a maiden named the Lorelei lives on the rock and lures fishermen to their death with her song." Well, that was nonsense. Lorelei must have thought the name was pretty. But why did she change her name at all, and if she had to, why didn't she stick with the letter J?

I loved our barn. It was my favorite indoor place in the world. I breathed in the clean smells of hay and, yes, manure. Earthy and real, it was wonderful! Lorelei never came there; she was afraid of horses. But I didn't want Amy to be.

"Look, Amy. This is my horse, Firefly. Firefly, this is Amy. She brought you a nice carrot." Firefly neighed appreciatively, although Amy stepped back.

"He's awfully big."

"He is a she," I said. "She's a lady, just like us. Go on, Amy. Give her the carrot." I'd call her Anna when others were around, but for now, using her right name was essential in getting her to relax and trust me.

Timidly, Amy held out the carrot, and then smiled in delight at Firefly's obvious enjoyment. "She likes it!"

"Of course, and she likes you, too. Now for the kittens." I led her to a corner where Nelly had given birth to three roly-poly balls of fur, now starting to develop their own personalities. "Be very gentle, so you don't worry Nelly."

All of Amy's reticence disappeared. "Oh, the dear, darling little things," she breathed. "I'll be very careful of your babies, Nelly," and she gave the mother cat loving strokes. Nelly showed her appreciation with loud purrs.

"You definitely have the right touch," I said. "Would you like to have one while you're here?"

"Yes! I'd like that one!" She pointed to a rambunctious gray fluff. "I'll call him Dusty. Can we take him inside?"

I shook my head. "Not yet. Nelly is still nursing her kittens. Dusty isn't old enough to leave his mother yet."

Amy teared up again, remembering. "I'm not old enough to leave mine, either."

I thought my heart would break.

December 12

Dear Kitty,

Today in English, we started to read *The Diary of Anne Frank*. Most of the guys did more bitching than reading. I mean, it's a depressing story about a girl. And it's December. Everyone would rather think about Christmas and presents and getting out of school. Who wants the Holocaust now? I kept quiet. It seemed kind of wrong—morally, you know—to complain when the author died such an awful death. Then I opened the book and nearly yelped out loud when I read "Dear Kitty." Anne Frank also wrote to a Kitty. Only her Kitty was a made-up friend. Have I made you up, too? Or are you out there somewhere wondering about me? Maybe you just died six years ago like everyone says.

I have biology homework. It's the same stuff we had in 8th grade.

Your brother,
Tim

"Looks like it's just the two of us," I told Amy. "I'm supposed to spend the weekend at the ranch with the other children, and they'll think it strange if I don't show up."

"Can I go, too?"

Well, that's what I had been wondering. "It all depends on how good you are at pretending."

"I'm good. My kindergarten and first grade teachers said I had the best imagination in our whole class."

I smiled. "This calls for a different kind of imagination. You would have to pretend that your name really is Anna and that Lorelei is your new mommy. And you'd have to act like you're happy here. You couldn't slip, Amy. If you want to go home again, you'll have to do what I say."

She nodded, even though I didn't think she could possibly understand. "Can't you just take me home now? I know my address."

That would be helpful in time. "How about your phone number?"

"Sometimes I do." She giggled. "I've never called myself before."

I laughed. The giggling was a positive sign. "That would be a strange thing to do. Before we can figure out how to get you home, though, I need to talk to Mark. He's the oldest and also a friend. He'll have some ideas."

"Couldn't we just tell the grownups? The ones at the ranch?"

So many times I'd thought about confiding in Leesa's parents. But I wasn't sure they'd believe me. The Dulows had known Lorelei far longer than they had me and considered her practically a saint. I sighed. Sometimes

I thought the whole town agreed with them. "I don't know," I said. "I'm afraid to take a chance."

Taking her to the ranch was risky, but so was staying here. But Amy promised to keep the bargain, and I hoped she could. After assuring her that Nelly would do a fine job taking care of her kittens, I lifted Amy onto Firefly's back, and then mounted behind her. "Hidden Jewel Ranch, here we come!"

Amy responded to the relaxed, accepting atmosphere of the Dulows' home. Fortunately, the adults were too busy with their own concerns to do more than greet her. She was not subject to embarrassing questions from them, and the children were—children. She seemed to fit right in with Kyle, Jenny, and Leesa's younger siblings, Kara and Norm. They and Bobby were mesmerized by a Disney movie on the large screen TV. Not needed at last, I dashed upstairs to Leesa's room, where I found her gazing helplessly at piles of stuff on her bed.

"Leesa, you are not going to take all that to Denver!"

"I know." She sighed. "But it's so hard to choose."

"I'll help." I plopped myself on a chair near the bed.

"About time you got here. What took so long?" She pushed over a stack of underwear and sat on the edge of the bed waiting, as if she knew I had to come up with something. "Well?"

"Well, Lorelei was called out of town suddenly. She phoned that she'd be gone for several nights, and Mrs. Benway—"

"Right. Mrs. Benway. Mark got a call from her and zipped out of here faster than Dynamite bitten by a horsefly. What was that about?"

"I have no idea," I said, truthfully. "All I know is that Mrs. Benway kicked her husband out and was so upset I told her to go home. I finally decided to bring Anna here. I couldn't just leave her alone."

"Anna's here? Where? How's she doing?"

"She seems okay. She's downstairs watching 'The Lion King' with the others."

Leesa grinned. "Kara and Norm have been glued to it since Mom bought the DVD. They've memorized all the songs. Dad and I are totally sick of it. But why would Mrs. Benway want to see Mark?"

I shook my head. It didn't make sense. Very little did. Time to change the subject. I pointed to her clothes. "Let's cut all that in half and then in half again. Then maybe you'll be ready to pack. But you're not going for at least a week, right?"

"Uh-uh. Plans have changed. Blanche's dad has a conference in Colorado Springs, so we're going Thursday morning."

"Before graduation?"

"Yes, but it doesn't really matter, does it? What's wrong, Kath?"

I might have been on the verge of a panic attack. Keep it together, I told myself. Breathe. Hang on until you can figure out what you're feeling. My voice shook, but I managed. "Nothing, really. I guess I just realized how much I'll miss you."

"You looked like it was more than that. I'll miss you, too, but we'll write. Remind me to give you the address this weekend."

"And the phone number. Be sure to give me the phone number." I don't know why, but all at once having it seemed essential. I felt alone, abandoned, with insurmountable problems: Mark off on some mysterious errand, Mrs. Benway gone, Amy needing to go home, dirt mounds in the woods, and the hardest problem of all to fathom—the change in Lorelei. But I needed to break the mood.

"Let's pack. You won't need more than a week's worth of underwear." I counted out seven pairs. "You sleep in T-shirts, so that's no big deal, and two bras should be plenty." Leesa sighed, but returned a lacy mass to a drawer. "Now pick out two party outfits, and that's all." She obeyed. "One pair of walking shoes, and one pair of dress shoes. Jeans, two pairs of shorts, and one bathing suit. Next, what will you need for work?" In this way, we wheedled down the stacks until they became manageable. Leesa loved clothes, and I didn't trust her not to add more as soon as she was alone. I insisted she put her selections into the large suitcase immediately. I slammed it shut. "There, all packed!"

She seemed bewildered. "That's it? Are you sure?"

"Positive, and knowing you, you'll find plenty to buy there."

She brightened. "That's true. Denver has lovely stores."

I gave her a hug. "You're hopeless." But if I had her kind of money, I might enjoy stores and shopping sprees, too. As it was, my jeans would do fine for practically every occasion. Of course I did have money, but that was different. I dared not use it for anything but emergencies. I wasn't sure why that was true, but I'd always known it was.

"Now what?" Leesa asked, once the clothes were out of sight, no longer a temptation.

I wanted to look for Mark but decided to wait for him to find me. I shrugged. "Maybe check on the children—I mean, kids—and if they're doing okay, take a ride or go for a hike."

"Dynamite needs exercise," Leesa said. "Good idea."

The Dulows' barn was far more spacious than ours, for this was a working ranch. They boasted twelve horses, counting Firefly and Mr. Tom. (Mark hadn't returned, judging from Mr. Tom's absence.) Donna, Leesa's mother, gave horseback riding lessons, and the whole family entered various competitions in the state, including events at the state rodeo.

We rode to my favorite outdoor place in the world, Curtain Call Gap, where I could look down into the canyon and miles beyond to the San Juan Mountain Range. Lisa and I dismounted and sat quietly, looking and breathing in the pine-scented air. To my dismay, I started to cry—silently, no sounds at all—I couldn't stop the tears rolling down my cheeks. I searched my pockets. Nothing there that would help.

Leesa handed me a rumpled tissue. "Kathy, you're one of my best friends, but I've never seen you cry before. What's wrong?"

That jarred away the tears. *One* of her best friends? She was my *only* friend! Although hurt, I tried to make light of it. "Oh, nothing. Allergies or growing pains, Mark graduating, you going away . . . We aren't children anymore, and I wish we could just stay the way we are right now."

Leesa shook her head. "I don't buy it. You've been unhappy for a while now. Are you in some kind of trouble? Are you . . . Oh, no! You and Mark . . . Are you—"

"Leesa, no! It's not like that. I mean, we use—"

"Ah ha! Then you and Mark have done it. You know, Kathy, we always said we'd tell each other when it happened."

I blushed furiously. But this conversation was a whole lot safer than other subjects. Lorelei was the topic I needed to avoid. "I know, but it's different when it's real. It's too private."

"Well, okay. I won't ask for a blow-by-blow description."

I winced. "What a way to put it."

Leesa giggled. "Maybe that didn't come out right. Just tell me what it was like. How did it feel?"

"Nice," I said feebly.

"Nice. Well, gee whiz, thanks. Sex feels nice. That gives me, your very best friend, something to look forward to. Can't you do better than nice?"

"Well, if it's with someone you care about—"

Leesa stood. "Guess I'll have to find out for myself. Shall I make it another Denver goal?" She began to laugh. "Nice," she hooted. "I can hardly wait!" Then she looked back at the path. "Speak of the devil!"

And there was Mark, riding up to meet us. Leesa spoke first. "Hey, Mark, we were just talking about you."

She wouldn't dare! I gave her a threatening look, but she didn't even look my way. "We were just wondering what Mrs. Benway wanted." She smirked at him.

What a tease! I'll get you later, Leesa, I warned silently, but I had to say something. "Yes, we were wondering. It seemed strange that she called you here." Or that she called—period.

Mark squirmed. He, too, was trying to figure out what to say, but lying was in our blood. He'd manage to be convincing. "I guess she tried the house, but no one was home."

"That must have been when Anna and I were in the barn," I said. He raised his eyebrows slightly at that. "No one is home. Lorelei is away overnight—maybe for the whole weekend—and I think Mrs. Benway quit. I brought Anna here. We're all here." That was the best I could do at explaining with Leesa listening, although she had mounted Dynamite again. Your turn, Mark.

"Yeah, the Benways are history. She threw her husband out and is going to live with her sister. She wanted to give me some papers she thought we might like to have—old school drawings, things like that—bound together with a festive ribbon, almost like a Christmas present. I didn't want them, but it was nice of her. Doubt if you'll want them, either."

I got it. Mrs. Benway never saved any of our drawings, but she must have confided in Mark and given him some papers—possibly ones that would help us understand more about what was happening. We'd talk later. Alone.

December 20

Dear Kitty,

Yes! I got my Christmas present early from Aunt Kay. I had assured her it was the only thing I wanted, and she came through. She has paid for and is allowing me to go on a school-sponsored ski trip to Chestnut Mountain Ski Lodge. It's pretty far north of here, near Galena. Because of you, Aunt Kay is scared to death of me going anywhere without "proper supervision." I guess she's decided that Sandburg's PE teachers will supply that. (Ha! If she only knew!)

Your old friend Lisa is going, but she'll hang out with her own pals, and they'll keep their noses higher than Chestnut Mountain. Doesn't matter. Lots of my friends are going. We'll be gone for five days, and I'm planning to make each day count.

No, I don't know how to ski. What does that have to do with anything?

Merry Christmas, wherever you are!
Brother Tim

THE MOVIE WAS OVER AND the children restless, badly needing to stretch and play. But Bobby demanded loudly that he wanted to see "The Lion King" again. Kyle agreed, perhaps to make Bobby stop, and Norm said he might as well watch it, too, since there wasn't anything else to do. Kara glared at Leesa and walked away in disgust.

Leesa shrugged. "A harbinger of summer. You're right, Kara. Mom won't like it, but I don't feel like arguing." She re-started the film, giving me a look that clearly said Bobby was becoming more and more of a problem—a huge baby who must always have his own way.

That left the younger girls, Leesa, Mark, and me. I introduced Anna/Amy to Leesa, who wisely didn't make a fuss of her. Amy seemed down, and I wanted to talk with her in private—to her and Mark. This was going to be tricky but Leesa and our own little Jenny came to the rescue. "Let's go play with the dolls, Anna. Kara has the biggest doll house in the world."

"Well, maybe not that big," Kara demurred.

"I need to check on some things," Leesa said, "and maybe you'd like to talk to Mark, Kathy."

I smiled thanks to my intuitive friend. I did want to, although not for the reason she was thinking. "Yes, Mark and I should get caught up on what's happening at home. I'd like Anna to stay with us for a few minutes. Then I'll take you upstairs to Kara's room, Anna. You'll love the doll house."

Kara and Jenny raced upstairs, with Leesa following. "Supper at six-thirty. Don't be late." That was directed at Mark and me.

After assuring Leesa we'd be punctual, Mark, Amy, and I went to the backyard, far away from any chance listeners.

Quickly, I filled Mark in on Amy's plight. Don't overreact, I urged him silently. He heard me. We'd been practicing silent communication for years. "So, the whole thing was a mistake," I said, "and we need to find a way for Amy to go home."

Mark knelt down and held her lightly by the shoulders. "I promise that you will, Amy. I understand that you're frightened, but you must continue to be brave and not let anyone know how scared you are."

Amy nodded. "Especially the bad lady. When will you take me home?"

"It will take some planning, but probably next Friday."

"That long? A whole week?"

"Yes, although we'll stay here at the ranch until at least Monday—maybe longer. You feel safe here, don't you?"

She seemed to be thinking it over. "Yes, they're nice to me."

I chimed in. "Just keep using your imagination. Pretend your name is Anna Harris and that I'm your sister, and Mark is your brother. We will try not to leave you alone with Lorelei, the woman who took you. Now, let's join the girls."

"One more thing," Mark said. "Where do you live, Amy?"

"Twenty-Four 4th Street," Amy said.

Mark smiled. "Do you remember what town?"

"Grand Junction," she said.

"Great. We can take the bus there."

Mark asked me to meet him in the barn, and Amy and I returned to the house.

The TV had been turned off, and Kyle and Norm had disappeared. Donna was sitting on the couch next to a pouting Bobby. What now? Didn't I have enough going on?

"Everything okay?"

Donna smiled at me, but only with her mouth. Her forehead was wrinkled, and her eyes didn't meet mine. "Bobby and I have been discussing proper behavior and language," she said. "I think we understand each other."

I understood but doubted that Bobby did. "Is there anything I can do?" I asked, hoping Donna would say no.

She did. "Bobby is going to help me prepare supper. We're going to have a good time, aren't we, Bobby?" He agreed, anxious for the scolding to stop. He trotted ahead to the kitchen. Donna stood. "We'll talk later, Kathryn," she said, before following him.

Not now or later, I pleaded to a God who had long ago deserted me. I couldn't deal with Bobby, too.

The horses had had enough of a workout for the day and had settled in to eat and rest. Mark and I walked into the woods adjacent to the ranch. He put his arms around me, but I broke away. Hurt, Mark stared down at his boots. "I am sorry, but there's no time. We've got to talk."

He sighed. "Yes, we do, unfortunately. Let's start with Amy, and then I'll tell you what I learned today."

Whatever his meeting with Mrs. Benway was about, I thought. "You told Amy you'd take her home Friday. Why then?"

"Graduation is Thursday night, Kath. I must be there for that, but I don't dare stay much longer. Thank goodness we won't have to go farther than Grand Junction. I'll take Amy home, and then leave for good. I want you to come with me."

"Me?"

He sat me down on a fallen log and turned my face to his. "I know you're scared, honey. I am, too. Shitless. But staying here is too dangerous."

"Lorelei needs me, Mark, and so do the others. Jenny is only twelve— she can't be in charge. Lorelei will be okay again. Mistakes can happen to anyone."

"You mean like kidnapping and murder? That kind of mistake? God, I hate that woman! All that loving and sweetness is a sick act. Can't you see the truth? She's about as sweet as a rattlesnake."

I could no longer deny that Lorelei was ill, but I still loved her—didn't I? "I guess the kidnapping did happen, at least twice. We weren't really kidnapped, though. I went willingly."

"Right. At the ripe old age of ten. Is that the new age of consent?"

I didn't respond. Instead, I flashbacked to a miserable little girl sitting alone in the airport, abandoned and longing for her father and little brother, completely resenting an aunt who had become the enemy. Yes, I had left willingly enough, but . . . I didn't want to remember. Not now.

"But murder?" I returned to the rest of Mark's accusation. "You mean David and Sarah? Mark, a couple of dirt mounds and a class ring aren't proof of anything. Besides, Lorelei couldn't have done it herself. She's not strong enough." Unbidden came the memory of Bobby and the shovel. Impossible. I wouldn't share that with Mark.

Mark walked away and stood, deep in thought. Then he returned and lifted me into his arms again. "Kathy, I went back to that spot. There was fresh digging—a new empty grave. Should I wait for proof, and then find out the hard way that it was meant for me?"

I gave up—no more denials. "Should you even wait until Friday?"

"I must. I need that diploma if I'm going to have a decent future."

Keeping my suspicions about Bobby had been wrong, so I told him about finding Bobby in the barn with the shovel. "He didn't say why he had it, but he seemed so proud of himself."

Mark whistled. "Lorelei could tell him anything, and he'd believe her. I don't know what's going to happen to Bobby. Mrs. Benway could control him, but not many other people can. About Mrs. Benway—"

I looked at my watch, a present from Leesa on my last birthday. "Mark, it's almost six-thirty. You'll have to tell me later." I gave him a quick kiss, and we raced back to the house.

Mark and I didn't have an opportunity to talk more that evening. After supper, dishes done, we all gathered in the large family room for board games. Because there were so many of us, several games were going at once, but the adults and older kids—Mark, Leesa, and I—separated into various groups in order to help the younger ones. Mark was with Amy, and I noticed him giving her conspiratorial winks. He seemed to understand that she needed reassurance that the pretending was only temporary.

Later, deciding where everyone should sleep was negotiated. Kyle and Jenny were used to bunking with Norm and Kara. Mark claimed Bobby, announcing that the two of them would use sleeping bags in the barn. I could tell the Dulows were relieved by this solution. So was I. I would have liked to stay close to Amy but knew this could cause problems with Leesa. Obviously, she wanted an overnight with "one of her best friends" and wouldn't understand having a little girl as another roommate. Amy would go with Jenny and Kara. At least she was tired, and it was doubtful she would stay awake long.

Probably I wouldn't either. The day had been as long as a week, I thought, as I crawled into the second twin bed in Leesa's room. That I had taken my last final only that morning seemed impossible. Suddenly it was summer, which had always felt like a new year to me—the start of wondrous changes—but I could no longer expect that. Happy New Year, Kath, I told myself. I could hear Leesa chattering, and then I could hear nothing, not even my own breathing.

January 3

Dear Kitty,

Happy New Year! Will this be the year I find you? I ask myself that question every year. Finals soon, but a lot of papers first. The semester paper, which I can use for both English and Social Studies, is on the importance of newspapers in society. I compared a few and wrote about what topics seemed to matter most to people, and which columnists I found most helpful. I also took a familiar case, your disappearance, and showed how various papers covered it. Most were respectful, but one suggested that Aunt Kay spirited you away so she could keep her brother-in-law's money. It was cruel, and you can imagine how upset Aunt Kay was. I have an ulterior motive in writing about newspapers. I heard that this summer an apprenticeship to work on a large one will be awarded to one or two students right here in Sandburg High. While it's unlikely that a freshman will be selected, you never can tell. It's important that I put myself out there, if you know what I mean.

So, I may not be writing to you for a while. I'm not enjoying these strange letters as much as I used to. Maybe newspaper work will take their place, or maybe I'll figure out how to write in a journal without it being about you. That's a thought!

Your brother,
Tim

CHAPTER NINE

I AWOKE BEFORE LEESA. SHE had always been a late sleeper if given the chance, but I needed total darkness. I'm wide awake the second the sun makes its first entrance. I looked at the lump on the bed, my best friend, and at the filled suitcase across the room. She would be gone in only five days. I wondered if I'd ever see her again. Of course I would! Why was I being so morbid? It's not like she'd never gone away before. But this time seemed different. I needed that phone number for the condo, in case her cell phone number wasn't enough. Here in the mountains, cell phones could be troublesome—either to place calls or receive them. Not that I'd ever had one, but I'd heard stories.

No sense in lying there. Fearful of the day and what new problems it might bring, I dressed quietly and tiptoed downstairs to the kitchen, where Donna and her husband, Hilliard, were drinking coffee. I thought I might have interrupted something important.

"Good morning," I said cheerily. "I seem to be first up, other than you, of course."

"Good morning, dear," Donna said, while Hill Dulow nodded. I'd always liked Leesa's father, but he was quiet and serious and somewhat hard to know. "Join us," Donna continued. "We'd like to talk with you."

I should have stayed upstairs. Problems already. "Is anything wrong?" Mr. Dulow poured me a glass of juice.

"Nothing you've done," he said quietly.

"It's Bobby," Donna said. "I'm afraid that we can't have him coming here anymore. If it were just Leesa, Hill, and me, that would be one thing, but he is not a good influence on the younger children. We want to help Lorelei, of course—my goodness, the woman's a saint—but she seems to be away from home more and more lately. I don't know the Benways; they haven't lived here long. Sometimes I wonder . . ."

"What did Bobby do?" I interrupted, hoping to prevent discussing Lorelei or the Benways.

"It's not just the foul language," Donna started. "I don't like it, but I suppose it doesn't do any real harm. But last night, Kara told me—" She stopped.

"Kara said Bobby pulled down her underpants," Mr. Dulow finished. "This is unacceptable, and when we talked to him about it early this morning, he didn't understand why it was wrong."

That was the thing, of course. Bobby didn't understand and never would.

"How old is Bobby?" Donna asked. And as I opened my mouth to give the stock answer, she said "Don't say fourteen. I know that couldn't possibly be true."

"I don't know," I said softly. "Do you want me to take Bobby home?" I would have to stay alone with him, but there was no other choice.

"That won't be necessary," Mr. Dulow said. "Donna will explain. I have to get to work."

Donna brought a box of cereal to the table and poured a bowl for me. I added milk, sugar—and waited. "Mark has taken Bobby to Mrs. Benway's," she said finally. "He called first. She agreed to take him for a few days, or at least until Lorelei returns. Mark says she's good with him. I never knew she was Lorelei's sister-in-law, did you?"

"Yes," I said. But I didn't say how recently I found out.

Donna handed me a folded note. "Here, Mark left a message for you. He'll explain. I've got to tend to the horses, so finish your breakfast. Try not to worry. None of this is your fault, Kathy. I've known Lorelei a long time, though not well, but my goodness, you and Mark, and Sarah and David before you, have been like members of our family." She gave me a quick peck on the cheek.

Not my fault, but my problem to solve. How soon would it be before Mark and I finally admitted we were in way over our heads? I opened Mark's note.

Kathy, our place a.s.a.p.

I ditched the cereal, gulped down the rest of my juice, and headed to the barn, hoping Donna wouldn't see me saddling up Firefly.

Mark was waiting in our cove. I wasn't too surprised to see he had brought along a sleeping bag. Well, that was all right, I guessed. First I needed some answers, I told him firmly.

He sighed, patting the sleeping bag, indicating we should at least sit down and be comfortable. "Okay, but it's a long, incredible story. I hardly know where to begin."

"Start with going to see Mrs. Benway yesterday."

He smiled ruefully. "Was that yesterday? It seems years ago." I knew exactly what he meant. "Well, it started in the office at school. I found out I was offered a college scholarship."

"Mark, that's incredible!"

"I agree. It's only for the first year, but it's renewable if I do well, and there are jobs available on campus. Well, the secretaries like me and were happy, too. Then I asked if I could see my file, to make sure the college had everything it needed. I've been a little worried about not having a birth certificate. There must have been one for me to start school here in the first place. And maybe I'll need one for college, too."

"And for driving," I added. I had Firefly and didn't care about a car but knew Mark didn't feel the same way.

"The secretaries hemmed and hawed a bit, but they couldn't see any reason why I shouldn't see basic stuff, so they let me look through my folder. There was a copy of my birth certificate, all right. Forged, but it looked authentic."

"At least enough to satisfy the school," I said, "but maybe not enough to pass a DMV inspection."

"That's what I think. Lorelei doesn't want anything to do with the Feds. But, Kath, I found something else. Lorelei's real name."

I nodded. "Mrs. Benway told me. I could hardly believe it. Josephine Grace Benway."

"I didn't know about the Josephine Grace part. The records said my parent was Lorelei Benway Harris and that my father, Mark Harris, was deceased. There was nothing about adoption. But the Benway part stopped me, so I called Mrs. Benway from school. She said she had nothing to say to me—then."

"Then she called you at the ranch?"

Mark nodded. "So I rode over and she gave me these." From his saddlebag, Mark pulled out papers—not cute little drawings—but legal-looking documents. He opened a few: Birth certificates, immunization records, a few adoption papers—all forgeries. "Mrs. Benway discovered them in her husband's desk. They're duplicates, and Mr. Benway is the forger."

"So now we know that part. Lorelei got her brother to help her. Do you think he helped her kill Sarah and David, too?" I had finally admitted it. Someone I loved was a monster. Sick, but still a monster.

Mark gave me a hug. He knew what saying that had cost me. "No, the helper was Bobby."

"The shovel. Did he tell you what happened?"

"Not in so many words. Last night I pointed to a shovel in the barn and said that sometimes I enjoyed digging holes but wished I were stronger so I could dig bigger ones. Well, he fell for it and said he could dig bigger and deeper holes than anyone."

"Smart. You can count on Bobby to brag."

"Then I said once I had to dig a hole to bury my pet dog and that I was very sad. I could tell he was trying to remember my having a dog, but he finally gave up and just agreed. Then I said that sometimes people get sick and die and that's even sadder."

"Oh, my God! Did he admit it then?"

"Good enough. He said 'Bobby is good at digging. He helps Mommy bury dead people.' He said sometimes he carries them for Mommy. He's certainly large and strong enough, but I don't think he murdered them. It must have been Lorelei. How, I don't know."

"And Bobby would think they just got sick and died, and he always wanted to help Mommy. That poor used mixed-up kid. What's going to happen to him?"

"I suspect that Mrs. Benway will take charge of him. She said what he needs is to be put into a school that can help him. Oh, almost forgot. Bobby actually is Lorelei's son."

"That explains a lot, especially why Mrs. Benway cares so much about him—her own nephew." We still had to worry about Kyle and Jenny, though, after Amy went home. Correction. I had to worry about them—and Lorelei. Mark wouldn't be there to help. Overwhelmed, I began to cry.

Mark's way of comforting was to open the sleeping bag. Making love seemed different and kind of wrong then, but I couldn't hurt Mark, even though I wasn't sure I wanted it to happen again. Before, we were living in a fantasy, a game, pretending we were just a normal teenage couple, a girlfriend and a boyfriend. But the fantasy was over, and it was time to face a grim, evil reality.

February 10

Dear Kitty,

Important announcement! I, Timothy Allen Hunter, have a girlfriend! It's as official as a freshman boy dating an eighth-grade girl can make it. I met her at the library where I was doing some research on climate change. She was writing a paper about rocks for her science class. I thought that sounded kind of boring, but she made it fascinating. Yes, she's a nerd like me. Her classmates call her Freckles, and they're not being complimentary. I told her that I thought her freckles were cute.

One thing led to another, and I invited her to our Valentine Day dance, "Hearts on Fire." She said yes, as long as it was okay with her parents. They said yes, as long as they could meet me first and be the ones providing transportation. Fine by me!

I'm smart enough to know this might not last very long, but for now I'm happy. What about you, Kitty? You're sixteen—seventeen next month—if you're still alive. Do you have a boyfriend?

Hope your heart is on fire, too!

Tim

P.S. Almost forgot. Her name is Betsy.

CHAPTER TEN

—

SUCH A CHANGE, NOT HAVING to worry about Bobby, although I wondered what we would tell Lorelei. Chores and Dulow family activities had consumed most of yesterday, keeping Mark and me from going to the mine. He could go there practically any time, except for early mornings when he helped Max the ranch hand, but I couldn't spend much time away from Leesa. I was her guest, and it wasn't fair to her. But luck was with me, for once.

"Oh, good, you're back," she said, still in pajama bottoms and T-shirt, as I entered the house after a long, after-breakfast ride. "Blanche called and wants me to go to her house to plan. I don't know what she means by that—"

"But you'll be her guest in Denver and think that you should," I finished for her. "It's okay, Leesa, I totally get it. And since I haven't heard anything from Lorelei yet, we'll probably be here tomorrow, too."

She hugged me. "You are such a honey. I should have known you'd understand. I told Blanche I'd have to talk to you first."

"Call her back and say it's okay." Blanche knew I was there; that was the only reason she'd insisted on seeing Leesa, but this time it was fine by me. Mark and I would be able to retrieve the briefcase after all.

After Leesa left, Mark and I decided it would be smart to have lunch with the others. The main meal at the ranch was at night, even on Sundays. Daylight was precious on working ranches. Evening meals came after sundown.

The children were chattering happily about the newborn puppies one of the ranch hands planned to show them. Even Amy was enamored by the prospect. She seemed almost happy, and I was proud of her for the effort she was making. I dreaded taking her back to Lorelei, but I couldn't think of that now. The plan was that Mark would take Amy home to Grand Junction Friday morning, and then disappear. At the moment, he was the one in the greatest danger, and the final steps were up to him.

Early afternoon, we finally rode to Hidden Jewel Mine. All the way there, Mark fretted that somehow the briefcase would be gone, but I wasn't worried. No one ever went into the mine, and it sounded as if Mark had hidden the briefcase in a safe enough place. At any rate, we'd soon know for sure—as soon as the horses took us to the bottom of the ravine to the opening.

Ignoring the *Keep Out* and *Danger* signs, we kicked aside dirt and rubble blocking the entrance. More since he'd last been there, Mark observed. Outside, some of the old wooden shacks and buildings remained. Inside were old furnaces and prospector tools—the only indications of a business that had made the early Dulows stinking rich. Seeking shining silver! What a thrilling time it must have been!

Mark reached down and picked up a small, gray-streaked stone. "Here, Kath, a lucky piece for you."

"Silver?" I shook my head. "Doesn't look like silver to me. Are you sure?"

"Not sure, but probably. Silver is rarely found as a pure form. Gray streaks in a dark rock are often the only hint. And, after all, this is a silver mine."

I looked around the cold, forbidding cavern with rotting boards barely keeping the dirt ceiling in place—easily ten degrees colder than outside— and could see other rocks similar to the one Mark had given me. "If there's still silver, why did the mining stop?"

He shrugged. "Probably not enough left to be worth the expense." Then he checked in back of the tools and breathed a sigh of relief. "Yes, still there."

Neither of us wanted to stay inside the mine, nor did we want to leave the horses unattended, so we took the briefcase and led them into a forest of ponderosa pine, where it was unlikely we'd be noticed. We sat on a soft blanket of pine needles, and I handed Mark the key.

"Before we open this, Kathy, I want you to tell me your name."

"My name? Kathryn, of course. You know that."

"No, tell me your real name. I think we should tell each other our names and how we got here."

I knew he didn't mean how we got to the woods today. I didn't respond immediately because it had been years since I had said it. Almost seven, as a matter of fact. I'd been programed not to say or even think it. "It's Katrina," I said softly. "Katrina Hunter, but people called me Kitty."

"Kitty. Not a big jump to Kathy. I prefer Kathy."

Well, I did, too. I would stay Kathy, and Mark would always be Mark to me. "What was your name?"

"Matt. Matthew Lawrence."

"A nice name," I said. Then I told him about that long-ago day at the airport. "I don't remember what happened after we left. I mean, how we got here . . ." Oddly, I'd never thought of that before. How did I get here? I knew it had taken two days.

"It sounds like your life might have turned out all right," Mark said, not noticing my sudden confusion. "I don't think mine would have. Lorelei never had to brainwash me, although she insisted on going through her normal routine—*Your name is Mark. I'm your mommy*—I went with her without a moment's hesitation." He paused, thinking. "How strange that I hate her now. I never liked, much less loved, her, but she might have saved my life."

Mark said he was an only child and that his parents were dead. He had been living with an abusive stepfather. "You've noticed the long scar on my back, Kath. A present from him—a badly healed whiplash."

"Mark!"

"Doesn't hurt now, but I knew there'd be more to come, so I ran. I was in a bus station, attempting to pickpocket a man's wallet when Lorelei found me. A good thing she did."

"How ironic that she saved your life and that now she plans to end it." I finally admitted out loud Lorelei's intention. I still cared about her but had decided she was sick. Crazy!

"Now for the briefcase," Mark said, "and let's pray it will help us figure out a way forward."

I knew there was plenty of money for Mark to make his escape with Amy. The hard part would be to get the two of them into town Friday morning. What interested me were the papers I had never examined—from fear and maybe just not wanting to know what they said.

Mark unlocked the suitcase and whistled when he saw all the bundled hundred-dollar bills. "Why in the world would your aunt be carrying so much, and what did she plan to do with it?" I shook my head. "Well, let's look through the papers."

There was my birth certificate, immunization records, and school report cards. "So your birthday was in March," Mark said, "Not June 8th, when we've always celebrated it. You've been seventeen for almost three months."

I nodded. "June 8 is my homecoming." Our birthdays were celebrated on the anniversaries we first came to Seguro Haven. I picked up a few letters. One was to the Boston relatives. I showed it to Mark. "I guess this explains the money."

"So your aunt believed in cash only. Lorelei does, too, but for a different reason. Hmmm . . . she was going to give you the briefcase to hand over to a Mr. Daniel Brooks to help with your 'upbringing.'" Mark made invisible quotation marks in the air. "Your share, according to her, of your father's estate. Awfully formal letter."

"Well, she didn't know him. I didn't either. I didn't even know his name until just now." Presumably Aunt Kay would have explained when she returned from her interminably long visit to the "powder room."

"I wonder what would have happened to you if Lorelei hadn't come along."

I shrugged. No sense in speculating. I opened the other letter and gasped. "Oh, I'd forgotten about this!" It was from a psychologist I vaguely remembered seeing. I had been withdrawn and hostile after Dad died, even a little mean. Lisa, my friend back in Galesburg, told me that I'd better watch it because her parents were thinking we shouldn't be friends anymore. The note was actually the psychologist's evaluation, saying it would be advisable to send me away for a while, either to a facility for problem children or, if possible, to a different family.

"Mark, I really was a problem. I loved Dad more than anyone, and I was mad at the world for taking him away. Maybe Aunt Kay didn't want to get rid of me. Maybe she didn't have a choice."

"And maybe you'll find out someday," Mark said. And then he held me for a long, long time, just for comfort.

Before we left, Mark suggested that he take some of the money. I agreed. "It might not be easy for us to get back when we need to." But I wasn't certain it was safe to leave the briefcase.

Mark thought it over. "Mine collapses are always a possibility, and the wood holding it up looks even more rotten than it did a few days ago."

He took five hundred dollars, putting most of it into his saddlebag. About a hundred went into his wallet. I didn't ask why. I put the rest of the money—I thought a couple thousand—into mine. I tore up the letters and old report cards but kept the birth certificate and immunization records. It was doubtful Lorelei would go into the barn where I'd keep the saddlebag. Her fear of horses was extreme. We threw the briefcase back into the mine, and with that gesture, I said a final goodbye to my father.

Back at the ranch, Donna was glad to see us. "Leesa hasn't returned from Blanche's, and the children are clamoring to go swimming. I just don't have the time to watch them."

"We'll go," I said promptly, but when Mark seemed uncertain, I added, "at least I will."

"Oh, good." She started away but turned back. "Almost forgot. I'm afraid you missed a call from Lorelei."

"Is she home?" Mark asked.

"No, and she wants you to stay longer. At first, I thought she would be back tomorrow morning, but then she asked about Bobby. When I said he

was with Mrs. Benway, she said she wouldn't return until sometime on Tuesday. She sounded different. Is something wrong?"

"I don't know," I said, telling the truth for once.

"Well, I'm meeting a class of beginners," Donna said. "I think maybe we'd better have a talk later."

"That's one talk we'll try to avoid," Mark said, as soon as Donna was out of earshot.

I agreed but wondered if someday Leesa's mother might be our best chance at getting help. Finally, Donna was starting to guess things were not what they seemed. "You don't want to swim, Mark?"

"No, you go. Max is taking the truck into town, and I thought I'd hitch a ride in and back with him." At my look, Mark explained. "I want to check out the bus schedule and buy the tickets. Kath, I think Amy and I might need to leave right after graduation—Thursday night, instead of Friday. I'm afraid the longer we wait, the harder it's going to be. We just have to figure out how we're going to get Amy into town because I'm starting to think it won't be safe for me to go home at all."

March 22

Dear Kitty,

Happy Birthday! Seventeen today. Hope you celebrate and have a great time. (Actually, I just hope you're still alive.)

Big news! Guess where I'm going this summer? Denver, Colorado! Isn't that amazing? Any place other than Galesburg would be fine with me. I thought it might be Chicago, the only city I've ever seen, thanks to you. (Only kidding, sort of.) I've won our school's newspaper apprenticeship—sort of a junior apprentice— for a large newspaper. I won't do much more than observe, but what an opportunity!

Aunt Kay is holding the reins tight. She's making noises about me going, but my dean had a conference with her and said I would become as messed up as Aunt Kay if she didn't let up. Okay, those weren't his exact words, but that's what he meant. Anyway, I'm going—probably by plane, which means I'll have to return to O'Hare Airport. Aunt Kay is not happy. Tough!

Remember how you always thought she liked me best? Right. Sure she did! Practically the only time she talks to me is to scold and warn me not to do something I want to do. "You know what happened to your sister," she says.

"No, I don't, and neither do you," I say, but she always spaces out about then. Your picture is on the piano. Sometimes she stares at it for hours. I'm not even in Denver yet but already wish I never had to come back here!

Yours,
Tim

WHILE THE LAST THING I wanted was go swimming, once I jumped into the pond—what the Dulows called the Old Swimming Hole—I realized it was exactly what I needed. Jumping, shouting, splashing along with the children—so much fun, just to have fun! I was only seventeen—in a few days or last March, depending on whether I was Kathy or Kitty—and summer vacation was here. Shouldn't that mean something?

Amy made an almost perfect dive off a low board. The rest of us cheered when she joined us, laughing with pure joy. "Anna, you're wonderful!" I said.

"I was on a junior swim team at home," she confided.

I took her hand and squeezed it. "You'll be back soon," I promised, whether or not I had any right to. "Mark is buying the bus tickets today."

"Beach ball volley!" Norm yelled out, so we quickly formed teams for a thrilling goofy game.

As soon as Amy and Mark left Thursday night, I vowed to find ways of helping Kyle and Jenny. And myself—or the newest grave in the woods could be for me.

Finally exhausted, we collapsed on our thirsty beach towels, although the sun would be more helpful in drying us out. I relaxed, able to turn off the chatter for a bit, until Kyle grabbed my arm and began nagging. "Kathy, Jenny and I want to go to camp, too! Norm and Kara are going. Why can't we go?"

I laughed. "The last time I looked, I wasn't your mother, but maybe you should tell me about it. What camp? When? Where? You know, details?"

So with more of them telling me than was helpful, I heard about the Dulow children going to church day camp, tomorrow morning through the end of the week. A bus would pick them up, returning around suppertime. "And there's a sleepover Thursday night." Jenny breathed in ecstasy. "I've never been on a sleepover my whole life!"

What do you call staying overnight here? I almost asked, but I knew what Jenny wanted—some of the exciting adventures her classmates had, instead of a pretend mother who always said no. But what a blessing it would be if Mark and I didn't have to worry about the children when we had so much else to settle.

"Please, Kathy?"

"But wouldn't you have to be signed up by now? With parent or guardian signatures and medical reports and . . ." Well, I didn't know what else. I'd been on a Brownie Scout camping trip back in Galesburg when I was eight, but I certainly hadn't been in charge of the details.

Norm and Kara didn't know, of course; their mom had taken care of it. But four sweet faces looked longingly at me. Only Amy seemed uncertain. "I'll ask Donna," I agreed.

Of course that was as good as a "yes" to them, and they chattered loudly how grand it was going to be—all talking at once, so no one could hear anyone clearly. I did learn that the overnight was going to be on church grounds in town. In town, not far away on graduation night, when Mark and Amy would make their escape—the camp might offer a possible way for that to happen. But whether or not Lorelei had returned, I truly had my doubts.

Donna, thinking it over before responding, was cautiously optimistic. "I'll give the camp leader a call," she said. "She's a friend of mine, so it's possible. Let's see—three additional campers from our house tomorrow and Tuesday, and then also going to an address close by for the rest of the week. I'll find out before we tackle the other issues."

I noticed Amy's quick intake of breath and shook my head slightly at her. If the camp would accept them, it would make the way forward relatively simple. Amy would already be in town when Mark needed them to disappear.

"Yes, Jean. Yes, I do know the family. I can vouch for them. Yes, that would be wonderful. I'm willing, and their brother Mark is eighteen. He can sign, also. This is a fine thing you're doing for our community."

Donna was rewarded with a sea of smiles when she hung up. "Yes, you may all go to camp. Now go play, and I'll settle the rest with Kathy." They scrambled.

"You go, too, Anna," I said to Amy, who was lagging behind. "It will be all right."

"Sweet child," Donna said, completely misreading Amy's reaction. "Well, we do need a signature giving permission, but she said that mine and Mark's would do temporarily." It would do permanently, I thought, but we'd deal with that when we had to. "And there's a fee, but I can lend the money until I see Lorelei again."

"Oh, I can pay," I said too quickly. Then I explained that Lorelei always left emergency money for us. Big lie. Never easy getting money from Lorelei. "How much is it?"

It was a bit steep for only five days—one hundred per child—but it included transportation, lunches and snacks, the swimming fee at the pool, and dinner and treats for the overnight.

"It's not a problem if you don't have it, dear."

Well, I had it, and I guessed I'd call this an emergency. My paying the fee was the only way they could go, and that was that. "I've got enough," I said. "Thanks, Donna. I'll ride home later and get the money and more clothing. Anna doesn't have much yet, but maybe some of Jenny's old shirts and shorts would work."

She smiled. "That I can handle. Norm is growing like a weed. His out-grown shorts and T-shirts are fairly unisex and should fit Anna just fine." She glanced at the kitchen clock and then out the window. "My eager group of teenage girls is reporting in for a hurdles lesson. Oh dear, they look entirely too eager. One more thing. Jean said that with more campers being added, they'll need another chaperone, an adult or an older teen for the overnight. I said you should be available. Gotta go. And it looks as if Mark is back. You can get him caught up."

Mark was back, and yes, we needed to get caught up.

Mark saw both the risks and the possibilities. "That will put all three of us in town on Thursday night. You, Amy, and me."

"I won't be able to go to your graduation," I said, although I didn't know how that would have been possible anyway.

"But you will be able to get Amy from the church to the bus stop by nine, which is when the bus leaves."

"And I can tell Lorelei that you and I are chaperones," I said. "We won't say a thing about graduation. If she ever knew the date, I don't think she'll remember."

"Or care. There may be problems we're not even dreaming of now, but this just might work."

We rode to the house. So much had happened since Friday, it felt like we'd been away for years. After packing camp clothes for Kyle and Jenny, I looked through Amy's possessions; she had arrived with nothing but the clothes she was wearing. I added an old stuffed animal puppy of mine that she might find comforting. We needed to talk alone, so that she would understand why she must go to camp, too. A small duffle bag that would fit next to my saddlebag worked for the clothing and the three hundred dollars for Donna. My money and birth certificate stayed in the saddlebag. Not the best place, perhaps, but I guessed it was safe enough.

Mark had two large bags, old ones belonging to Lorelei. It looked like he was taking everything. "Mark?"

"You'll have to carry one for me, Kathy. We'll ride to the grove now and leave my stuff there. It's not supposed to rain tonight. Tomorrow, we'll take them to town."

"To town. Where, Mark?" He really was leaving. He would never return to our home, where Kyle, Jenny, Amy, and I would go Tuesday afternoon.

"A cheap motel. I might need more money."

"What if someone sees you?"

"Doubtful. No one we know goes to that part of town, and the manager won't care as long as the money is paid up front. I'll check in tomorrow. You'll have to cover for me with Lorelei."

I nodded. A more accurate word was lying. I was good at that.

Leesa came back from Blanche's shortly before dinner. A festive, happy affair—steak on the grill, baked potatoes, corn on the cob, salad, and chocolate cake. Everyone was hungry and did more eating than talking, although Leesa was plenty excited about her upcoming grand adventure, and the children even more so about camp. Mark and I were silent and unnoticed. I wondered briefly how Bobby was doing but thought he was probably better off with Mrs. Benway. She loved him and could handle him. Digging holes, carrying dead bodies, and pulling down girls' underpants must not be Bobby's future.

Before the children went to bed—early so they would be ready for the eight o'clock pickup—Amy and I managed to talk privately. She nodded. "I'll go home with Mark Thursday night, but won't people at camp know I'm gone?" She was no dummy.

I'd thought of that. "I'll say you weren't feeling well and that Lorelei came to pick you up." I'd stay over, and Lorelei wouldn't know anything was wrong until the following afternoon. Then, to my surprise, Amy threw her arms around me.

"Do you want to come with me? My mama would help you."

I hugged her back, wanting to cry. "That's sweet of you, but I need to stay with Kyle and Jenny."

"Okay, but what do I say when Mama and Daddy ask what happened?"

An excellent question! When Georgia left, I warned her not to say anything, but this time . . . "Amy, I'm going to let you decide that," I said, astonishing myself. "You must do what you think is right." I didn't think I could protect Lorelei anymore.

"I love you, Kathy."

My eyes filled. "I love you, too, Amy."

April 30

Dear Kitty,

Not much longer before school is over, and I leave for Denver. Time is going to fly, so I may not be writing to you before then— or maybe not ever! Or, like Anne Frank, I shall consider Kitty my imaginary friend—just a way to make my journal entries more personal. I am furious with you right now, if you want to know the truth. I'm pretty mad at your old friend, Lisa Manion, too.

She's always pleasant when she sees me, but yesterday she stopped by my table at lunch and said she'd heard I was going to Denver and needed to talk to me. We agreed to meet for a Coke after school. The guys heard, of course, and boy, did I get it! Lisa is seriously hot, the most popular girl in the junior class. I'm okay, but not in her league.

So after school, we met at Charlie's. Lisa was waiting in a corner booth and seemed really nervous. Why, I couldn't imagine. "I heard you're Sandburg Gazette's representative in Denver," she said. "Congratulations."

I sat across from her. She already had two Cokes for us.

(I'm going to try to record the conversation accurately because my teacher told me to work on dialogue.)

"Look, Tim," she said. "This is hard. I guess I'm only telling you now because you're going to Colorado. I should have said something years ago, but . . ."

That was weird. I told her to go on.

She pulled a letter from her purse and handed it over. Not an envelope—just a piece of wrinkled, lined notepaper. It's a good thing I was sitting down. Well, you know what was in it, don't you, Kitty? It was from you, written almost seven years ago.

Dear Lisa, don't tell anyone! I am okay. I have a new home and a new mother. I am going to be happy here, so don't worry. I'll never forget you.

Love, Kitty.

Lisa didn't tell anyone! Not even the police when they questioned her. Obviously, I let her have it. But she claimed the note had come after the police left and that she was "too scared."

She was scared? Aunt Kay still isn't okay. She thinks you were kidnapped and murdered for the money. Lisa could have given us hope and saved the police hours and hours. She might have preserved Aunt Kay's sanity—not to mention what her silence has done to me.

Lisa was only ten, and you were her best friend, and you asked her not to tell, so she didn't. I suppose that's the way little kids think. "Well, you haven't been ten for a long time," I said. But I stopped scolding; it wouldn't have done any good.

She no longer had the envelope but remembered the postmark said somewhere in Colorado—"Something Heaven in Colorado."

So that was why the big revelation—because I'm going to Colorado. It's a big state, I pointed out, but maybe I'd find something. Better late than never, I guess. I thanked her but didn't finish my Coke, and I took the letter with me.

Should I show Aunt Kay or the police? After all this time, I don't know what good it would do. Maybe I can find *Something Heaven*—obviously not the name of a real town, but perhaps something similar. Working in a newspaper office will be a good place to begin.

For the first time, I've got to wonder how innocent you were, Kitty. Did you leave deliberately? If so, how? You were only ten, too. I'll try to remember Lisa's feeble defense and apply it to you. Suddenly, this trip is taking on a whole new purpose.

Tim

I AWOKE EARLY TO HELP the children get ready for the bus and to be sure they ate a good breakfast. Donna and her husband were at their ranch chores already. Mark came inside to help and grabbed Kyle and held him high. "Let's take another look at that shirt, buddy!"

Kyle squirmed but finally allowed Mark to take off his shirt and turn it right side out. He didn't think it mattered, but it would if anyone laughed at him, Mark observed.

As soon as the bus pulled out, with all five children contributing to an almost-full busload, Mark and I looked at each other and nodded. While Leesa was still asleep and the adults occupied, we saddled up Firefly and Mr. Tom and returned to the grove to pick up Mark's bags before taking a back route into town.

Mark wanted me to go inside his motel room. He raised his eyebrows up and down, sort of his naughty way of signaling his intentions, but I shook my head. "No, Mark. We're not going to cheapen what's good between us in a run-down motel."

"Okay," he said reluctantly.

"Besides, it would be better for me to stay hidden with the horses. Why take a chance that anyone will see them alone." I handed him another hundred-dollar bill. "Just in case," I said.

"Thanks. Someday I'll pay you back for everything, Kath."

"I'm not worried about the money. It's never felt like it belonged to me, anyway. It's just . . ."

"You're worried we won't be together again?"

"Of course."

Mark wasn't in the room long, although it seemed an eternity to me. What if I were spotted? For once, I couldn't come up with a convincing story. On the ride back to the ranch, we agreed that I should spend the day with Leesa and that he should help with chores. "I need to figure out how to get back to town tomorrow," he said. He would not be returning. After tomorrow, I wouldn't see him again until Thursday night, and then it would be to say goodbye.

After cooling down the horses and leading them to where they could graze, Mark and I parted, he to the barn and me to the house to search for Leesa. But as I was entering the back door, Blanche was heading out, crying.

Momentarily, I forgot we weren't friends. "Blanche, what's wrong? Why are you crying?" I must have sounded as sincere as I felt because she forgot we weren't friends, too.

"Everything is wrong," she sobbed. "For one thing, my grandma in Idaho just died. I really loved her."

Hard to believe, but I hugged her. That's what you do when someone is suffering, and you don't know how else to help. "Blanche, I am so sorry!"

"Thanks," she muttered, pulling out of my embrace.

"I never knew my grandparents," I said. "I don't even know if I have any, so you're kind of lucky. I would have liked some, even if it meant losing them one day."

Blanche stared at me. "Oddly enough, that helps, Kathy. I don't know if I'd ever think of that, so thanks." A car pulled into the drive. "It's my dad to pick me up; I'm boarding my horse here. We're flying out of Cortez. You'd better go inside and talk to Leesa. This messes up her plans, too."

Of course. If Blanche and her family were going to Idaho, it probably meant her relatives in Denver were going, too. Leesa wouldn't be able to stay at their condo.

She was in her room pacing. "Leesa," I said, "I just heard. Poor Blanche, but what are you going to do?"

"I don't know," she wailed. "I'm trying to think, but my brains aren't working. I've got the apprenticeship, but now no place to stay."

"Blanche's family won't be in Idaho long. Maybe you can just stay in a hotel until Blanche and her sister return."

Leesa shook her head. "That's what I thought, but Blanche says they'll stay at least until the end of June. Guess Grandma was wealthy, and there will be all kinds of complications with the will."

"Sounds cold," I said.

"It does, but Blanche did love her grandmother." That had been my impression, too. "Oh, Kath, I just can't give it up. What shall I do?"

"First wash your face. Then we'll go find your mom." As I was learning more and more, Donna was good at problem solving.

She was between classes, taking a break, so the interruption came at a good time. We grabbed Cokes and sat at the kitchen table to brainstorm. "Well, we can't have you staying alone in a hotel room for the summer," Donna said. "It's not just the expense—I would be nervous you weren't safe."

"It wouldn't be much fun, either," Leesa said glumly.

"Let's give Miss Stratton a call." Donna went to the bulletin board where a long list of phone numbers was posted. The journalism teacher didn't pick up, so Donna left the ranch number and a detailed message. "We'll wait and see," she said, before hurrying to the next riding lesson.

"We'll wait and see," Leesa repeated. "Swell."

That meant we couldn't go anywhere. "So we stay right here near the phone," I said. "Won't be the worse thing that's ever happened. Seems funny not to have anything to do, though."

Two best friends, who suddenly had very little to talk about. I was jeopardizing our friendship by keeping the most important things about me private. But there was too much at stake until Mark and Amy were gone, then we'd see.

"I wonder how they're getting along at camp," I said, after a long silence. "Especially Anna."

"It's amazing how quickly she adjusted. You'd think she'd been here for months, not a week."

Only a week. Probably the longest one of my life.

"What's her story, Kath?"

"Story?"

"You know, what was her life like before she got here? What happened to her parents?"

I shook my head. "Lorelei said she's an orphan." That wasn't a lie; it was what Lorelei had said.

"I don't suppose you can ask Anna about it yet."

And we were silent once more, waiting. Finally, thankfully, the phone rang.

I couldn't tell much from what was mainly a one-way conversation. Miss Stratton was doing most of the talking. But gradually, Leesa began to smile and then she started to sparkle. "Oh, thank you, Miss Stratton. Yes, grab it; I know my parents will approve. Mom is teaching now. Can she call you later? Okay, thanks. Bye."

Leesa whirled me around the room. "It's going to great, Kath! Maybe even better. I just have to figure out how to get to Denver, that's all."

That sounded like a lot to me, but Leesa seemed confident once more. "So tell me," I demanded.

"A girl dropped out, so there's a vacancy in one of the dorms at the university. I'll have a roommate and everything!"

"Just like you were in college already." I had to admit it did sound better than staying with Blanche at her adult sister's condo. "Next step—Blanche's father was going to drive, so you are without a way to get there," I said.

"Right. Do you think Mom and Dad would let me drive myself?"

"Doubtful, but you can always ask."

"This is a Dad question," Leesa said. "Gotta find him!"

I was happy that the new problem was on its way to being solved, but it wasn't going to make any difference to me. Somehow, with an amended plan, Leesa would go as scheduled, and soon the rest of the Dulow family would be away on vacation. I would remain, alone with Lorelei, and responsible for the care of Kyle and Jenny. I was too young, and suddenly too tired. Would it ever be my turn for fun?

June 3

Dear Kitty,

Yeah, I'm writing to you again. Sorry about skipping May. Wasn't just mad; had heaps of work to do.

Tomorrow I leave for Denver, heading for fun, adventure, and the "educational experience of a lifetime" (according to the brochure) with Mr. Robbins and a few other students from East Galesburg and Henderson. Their advisors couldn't make it, so we're all going in Mr. Robbins' van. Road trip! Aunt Kay is so relieved I'm not flying that she's close to approving the whole venture. We plan to be there by Thursday night, so we can sign in first thing Friday morning. Mr. R. says we'll take our time and see the sights along the way. I've never done anything like this before and am so excited. I'm glad that I'll get to know the boys, too, because I might be rooming with them. We'll be staying in dorms at the University of Denver.

Aunt Kay had been stewing like crazy until her sister called and invited her to Detroit for the summer. She agreed only after I nagged her to death. We don't get along that well, but she has taken care of me for a long time. I told her I was grateful but that she deserved a life, too. I think we finally heard each other!

I might have had another breakthrough about—You! I wasn't getting anywhere searching the Internet for towns in Colorado that had the word "Heaven" in them. But yesterday, I got a list of all the apprentices that will be working and observing at the Denver Times this summer. I might have found the place. A girl is attending from the town of Seguro Haven, Colorado. Haven—Heaven? Maybe. Weird name, but an article on the web said seguro is Spanish for safe. Of course it's a long shot. Even if it was the town where you mailed the letter, that doesn't mean you're there now. But I will find this girl, Leesa Dulow. Another Lisa. Wouldn't that be a weird coincidence? Back to packing.

Your brother,
Tim

I‌N SPITE OF LEESA'S PLEAS, both sensible and preposterous, her parents refused to consider letting her drive to Denver. Instead, her father would have the honor of taking her early Thursday morning. The new plan of living at the university had been approved immediately. In fact Donna said the supervision most likely would be better than at the condo. "And transportation to the newspaper easier," she added.

I thought it strange that one newspaper could handle so many students, but Leesa explained that they would be divided among many newspapers in the area. Some were in towns outside of Denver, including Colorado Springs, some distance away. The university was just housing those apprenticing at the Denver Post and other Denver papers. "Here's a list of everyone. Students are coming from all over the country."

I muttered appreciation at her name under the D section but didn't look further. Not interesting. Besides, I could hear the bus in the driveway. Home from camp!

And a messy, exuberant, exhausted bunch they were! Jenny proudly wore a bandage on her finger, a souvenir from carving a horse figure out of soap. This she gave to Donna, who said it was one of the nicest presents she'd ever received. "Don't use it taking a bath," Jenny warned.

Donna smiled. "I won't. But speaking of baths—before supper. Now! All of you!"

All five were hustled upstairs to take turns using the two available bathtubs. Amy lingered behind. "Did you have a good time, honey?" I asked.

She nodded. "The kids and counselors are nice. I painted a picture for you, Kathy, but it isn't dry yet. I'll give it to you tomorrow."

"That will be something to look forward to," I said.

It would be the only thing about Tuesday to look forward to.

The next day, after we talked with the bus driver about dropping our three—Kyle, Jenny, and Anna—off at our house instead of the ranch, Mark and I were alone, wondering what to do. Mark, of course, suggested going to the grove, but I said no. "Let's take the horses to Curtain Call Gap. That's special, too."

"You don't want to be with me anymore, Kathy?"

"It's not that, exactly. It's hard to explain. I do love you—more than anyone. But we're too young, and you're going away, and we may never see each other again. And I'm going to be here, dealing with I don't know what. I'm scared, and I don't want to complicate things any more than they are now." I started to cry. He had to go, but how would I manage without him?

He nodded, no longer hurt. "I think I understand. Yes, let's ride to the lookout. That is a special place for us."

We sat on the cliff ledge, a surprisingly grassy area. The horses were loosely tied to trees not far away. Loose enough so they could reach down and munch the sweet grass.

"Mr. Tom will miss you," I said, and then wished I hadn't. Mark looked so sad.

"I'll never see him again, or this view. Nothing will ever be as beautiful as this place, that horse, or you."

I tried to make light of his words, fearing more tears. "In that order?"

He laughed. "I don't know about the place or the horse, but we'll be together again."

"You never told me, Mark. What school offered you a scholarship?"

"Northern Arizona in Flagstaff. Grand Junction is the wrong direction, but that's okay. I'll take my time getting to Flagstaff, even though I don't think Lorelei will come looking for me." No, probably Lorelei would pretend he'd never existed or make up some plausible story. "The high school sent my transcripts already and will send the final one soon. I took my birth certificate and immunization records. Forged or not, I figured they belonged to me."

"Will you have enough money?"

"I won't take more from you, Kath. I'm handy. I'll find some odd jobs right away and then get work at the university. Lots of kids do."

He put his arm around me and we cuddled close. Both of us were hurting, but finding the right words was hard.

"You'll ride home before the bus comes?" he said finally.

I nodded. "Whether or not Lorelei has returned. None of us wants to leave the ranch."

"But you must because of my cover story. I feel bad about that, but the Dulows have to think we've gone home."

Mark said he'd grab a ride into town with Max right after lunch and say that a friend would drive him home. Actually, Mark would spend two and a half dreary days in the grubby motel room—leaving cautiously for a few meals—until it was time for him to get ready for graduation. Graduation—a time when his whole family should be together to applaud the class valedictorian and celebrate his achievement. But Mark would be alone because a woman the town considered his saintly mother planned to kill him.

I shook my head. "Mark, even if we did tell someone, would anyone believe us?"

He smiled gently, and then gave me a long kiss goodbye.

Lunch would have been a silent affair if Leesa hadn't been so excited about going to Denver. Donna and I engaged in a fruitless argument with her about not needing to pack additional clothing. "But I'll need more now," she insisted. "Who knows what the laundry facilities are like?"

"You can wash out your underwear," I said.

"Yuck!"

"My spoiled, oldest daughter," Donna said good-naturedly. "I will give you plenty of coins for the washer and dryer. A dorm that large is certain to have plenty."

Leesa stared longingly at the backstairs leading up to her room. Donna and I winked at each other. Both of us knew that nothing we could say would dissuade her from packing as much as she could until the suitcase was barely manageable.

Mark stood and picked up his dishes. "Please excuse me, but I'd better git if I'm going to catch a ride into town. I'll see you back at the house, Kathy." He said it airily, as if it meant nothing. He took his dishes to the sink while Leesa made her escape. Then he turned back to the Dulows. "Donna and Hill, thanks for having us here. In fact, thank you for everything."

Careful, Mark, I warned silently. You sound way too solemn. But the Dulows didn't pick up on it. Time for them to get back to work. I offered to do the dishes. Why not? I didn't have anything else to do.

Then I was alone. Might as well go back to the house, I decided. I needed to be there when the bus arrived. If Lorelei returned first, I would explain about the church camp before the children were there to confuse things further.

Lorelei was not there. The rooms were exactly as Mark and I had left them. But everything felt different—no longer like home, more like a haunted house—so I returned to the barn. At least I'd have Firefly, Nelly, and her kittens for company. Poor neglected Nelly. First, I filled her food and water dishes, and then stretched out on a pile of hay to stroke the sweet balls of fur and breathe in the good barn smells. If only we could have stayed one more night at the ranch, but Lorelei was bound to return and Donna about to ask the impossible-to-answer questions I saw forming in her eyes. We might need your help someday, Donna. Then I didn't do much thinking, just listened to Firefly crunching her oats, Nelly's purrs, and the kittens' sucking sounds as they enjoyed an early supper. Nelly's babies were taking a lot out of her, and she was becoming thin. The rest of us needed to take better care of her, now that Bobby had left. I needed to take better care of everyone. The person who wouldn't receive care was Kathy. Stop it! Self-pity would not help.

The bus arrived. At least I wouldn't be alone.

Once again, the children were tired, dirty, and hungry. This time, it was up to me to fix supper; I almost missed Mrs. Benway. Fortunately, I found a box of Kraft Macaroni and Cheese and discovered that the milk wasn't quite sour. "Wash up the best you can," I directed, "and then come down to eat." Wisely, they didn't object. They could tell I was every bit as tired as they.

Proudly, Amy handed me her painting. "I made it for you, Kathy," she whispered, "but maybe I should give it to that lady. Maybe it will help."

She meant Lorelei, of course. Her picture showed all of us: Lorelei, Bobby, Mark, Jenny, Kyle, herself, and me, against a mountain backdrop. I was touched. "I think that is a very good idea, Anna." She nodded, realizing I didn't want anyone to hear me say Amy.

Late that night, I awakened with a start. Coming from the end of the hall, I heard sounds. Sounds coming from Lorelei's room. So she had finally returned. Then, to my horror, I heard a baby's cry, that special cry only infants make. Lorelei had not returned alone. A baby! Oh, no, Lorelei! No! No! No!

June 4

Dear Kitty,

We are on the road to Denver. Well, not exactly on the road. We're at a motel next to the highway in Omaha, Nebraska—it's kind of the halfway point to Denver. We didn't make many stops today because it was raining and Mr. Robbins decided to put some miles behind us. He's doing all the driving, so it's his call. It's supposed to be nice tomorrow, so maybe we'll stop and explore some then.

I should be asleep, but the guys are snoring so loudly I don't have a chance. Not yet, anyway. I don't know them well enough to say cut it out. They're a happy bunch, and don't seem to mind that I'm younger. Mr. Robbins is hysterical outside of school. He cracks jokes and makes us sing along to the corny cowboy songs he keeps playing on the CD player. "Git along little dogies" we sing at the top of our lungs. Dogies are cows, not dogs. Bob, one of the boys, yodels after we finish the "Whoopie Ti Yi Yo" part.

This trip is going to be good for me, and I hope Aunt Kay's visit with her sister helps her, too. We care about each other, but we need more people to matter to us.

Lisa came to the house to say goodbye. She's been kind of sheepish when she sees me. I told her I don't blame her, even though that's not the truth. Okay, she was only ten, but that's old enough to know when things are serious. She should have said something years ago. But I guess if I ever see you again, Kitty, I will forgive you. I think I'm ready to sleep now. Maybe I can snore and bother them.

Tim

CHAPTER FOURTEEN

URGING QUIET, I AWOKE THE children. "Mommy returned late last night," I whispered. "She'll want to sleep in." I was uncertain if the baby would "sleep in" and prayed that Lorelei hadn't drugged the poor thing. It was entirely possible.

All three dressed quickly. They carried their shoes downstairs, not making any sounds. I was not surprised to see Amy worried, but for the first time I noticed fear in Kyle's and Jenny's eyes. Perhaps they weren't oblivious to the danger, but more likely they were afraid Lorelei wouldn't let them go to camp. I made short work of breakfast, and then led them outside to wait for the bus. Curiously, they didn't question why Mark wasn't with us. I sensed their relief when the bus pulled up. I envied them. I wished I could escape, too.

I returned to the kitchen for a quick cup of coffee. Amy had propped up her painting near Lorelei's place at the table. "To Mommy," she had written on a post-it note, "Love, Anna." God! Mark needed to get her back before she turned into as good a liar as the rest of us. But it was shrewd on Amy's part and could be helpful.

In the barn, I watched Nelly and Firefly eat. I wanted to see Leesa, but she wouldn't be up yet. Even more, I wanted to see Mark, but going to the motel would be too dangerous. It would be a long day for me and even longer for him. "Firefly, it's just you and me. Let's go for a ride." But where, I didn't know. We needed food. I took a little money out of the saddlebag. "We'll go to the store, Firefly." Maybe I could put the food away before Lorelei noticed and wondered where we got the money. Or maybe she wouldn't even think of it. It had become impossible to know how she would react to anything.

When I returned at eleven, she still hadn't come downstairs. I was concerned about the baby, but there didn't seem to be anything I could do, other than hope it was still alive. I put the eggs, milk, butter, bread, and ham slice in the fridge. There was some cheese left. Maybe toasted cheese sandwiches for lunch—for Lorelei and me. And then . . . And then . . . And then I had an idea. Nelly needed a break from her kittens, who seemed to be thriving well enough. In fact, they were literally eating her out of house and home. I'd bring them inside for a while. Lorelei seeing me playing with them would seem homey and childlike enough. I would show her the one Anna wanted to keep. All very innocent. I found a low box, lined it with a soft towel, and took the box of kittens into the living room.

And that's where Lorelei found me, playing with three fluffy creatures—just like a little girl. "Mommy!" I shouted in pretend delight. "You're home at last!"

Then I saw the bundle in her arms and jumped up, pretending I knew nothing about a new baby brother or sister. "Oh, Mommy," I whispered. "How precious. How wonderful."

Proudly, she loosened the blanket and showed me a sound-asleep infant. "Oh, I mustn't wake him . . . or her."

"He's a little boy, Kathryn. I'm happy that you're pleased." She sat on the couch. "Don't worry about waking him. I wish he would wake up. He's been asleep too long."

"I guess babies do need lots of sleep." I wondered how large a dose she had given him.

"They need to eat, too," Lorelei said. "I shall try to awaken him for a feeding as soon as you and I get caught up."

That I would try to stall. "Where did you find him, Mommy?"

Real tears came into Lorelei's eyes. Did she believe her own stories? "The saddest thing, Kathy. I found him in a dumpster. I was walking by an alley and heard the most plaintive cry. I thought it was a kitten." She smiled at the little rascals chasing each other around the room. "A newborn baby. Can you believe anyone would be that cruel?"

Well, I did believe people could be that cruel, but not this time—not to this baby. The cruelty belonged to Lorelei, for this was a healthy baby boy—if Lorelei's drugs hadn't nullified that—not a newborn. My heart bled for his parents, out there, somewhere. But there was nothing I could do right now. "Have you named him?" I asked.

Lorelei shook her head. "I don't have any letter to start with. You name him, Kathryn. That's your job."

"Hmm . . . and an important job it is. I know, we'll start at the beginning. Little man, your name is Adam."

Lorelei's face lit up, and she gave me the warm smile that used to make me feel so cherished. But something was different in her eyes—something unfocused, confused, troubling. "That is the best name of all!" she cried. "And someday soon, little man, I shall find you a little Eve."

It wasn't going to stop. It was never going to stop—unless I stopped it. But Mark and Amy must be the next big step. "That would be nice," I said lamely.

Finally she noticed. "Where are the children?"

"At day camp," I said calmly, as a matter-of-fact. "They'll be home around four, absolutely starving. We'll have an early supper."

"Camp?" Her voice was shrill. "All of them?"

"With Norm and Kara Dulow. Didn't Donna tell you on the phone? She made the arrangements. And they're having such a good time. Anna painted you a picture. It's in the kitchen."

"Anna?" She sounded completely bewildered.

"Yes, she's having the best time. Even more so than Kyle and Jenny."

"Oh." Lorelei stopped to think. "Well, I suppose it's all right. Adam will require my attention."

"I think he's starting to wake up," I said, hoping that was true. "How about I fix you and me some lunch? It's good to have you home, Mommy." I escaped into the kitchen, where I noisily crashed the pots and pans. I couldn't have stayed in the living room one more second. I just couldn't!

I heard her singing—or at least crooning—as she climbed the stairs. I assumed that bottles, formula, and diapers were in Lorelei's room. I put bread, cheese, and butter on the counter and was selecting the right-sized fry pan when I heard a tiny meeow coming from the vicinity of my left foot. "Dusty, I forgot about you. Do you miss your mama, too? Well, let's find your siblings and go back home." Fortunately, the other kittens had heard my voice and decided to join us. Back in the barn, an anxious Nelly had enjoyed her break and was ready to return to maternal duties.

With sandwiches prepared, I waited for Lorelei. The bread had browned perfectly, and I was hungry. Finally, I sat and ate my share. I could always stay and keep her company. But her sandwich was getting cold, and I was worried about the baby, so I climbed the stairs and rapped softly on Lorelei's door. No answer. I peeked in. She was sitting in a rocking chair, holding Adam—an empty bottle on a small table next to the chair—both asleep. Careful not to wake them, I transferred the baby to his improvised bed—one of Lorelei's large bureau drawers—and returned to the kitchen.

I covered the sandwich and left a note about not wanting to disturb her and placed Amy's painting where it couldn't be overlooked. Dishes done and put away—what next? Just wait, I guessed. Kill time. Wait for the next shoe to drop. Waiting. Always waiting.

Apples! That's what I'd do. A small basket remained in the fruit cellar. Homemade applesauce would go perfectly with the ham slice. Could I make biscuits, too? No, better not attempt too much. Bread and butter would do. A fine dinner the children would appreciate, whether or not Lorelei joined us. I wondered what Mark would eat that night.

We were all seated at the table ready to devour my efforts when Lorelei arrived, without baby. The children were pleasant in their greetings, but a certain reserve was present that I'd never sensed before. Only Amy rose to the occasion. Proudly, she handed Lorelei her creation. "Look, Mommy, I made this for you. See? I drew Bobby, Mark, Kathy, Jenny, Kyle, and me—Anna! The painting is a little sloppy because I'm a beginner. Do you like it?"

I shuddered. She was too good. A promising acting career might await her, but I finally understood the word "befuddled." Lorelei was beyond confused or puzzled; she was befuddled. She looked at Amy as if she'd never seen her before.

"Don't you like it, Mommy? I made it just for you."

Finally, Lorelei hugged the little girl and resumed the appropriate role. "Oh, my yes. I love it. I'll keep it always. Thank you, Anna." Seemingly satisfied, Amy returned to her meal.

Lorelei studied the painting while picking at her food. "Mark," she said urgently. "Where's Mark? Why isn't he here?"

I should have anticipated the question and was struggling with a response when Jenny piped up. "He's helping Max at the ranch. He told us at breakfast. Some of the fences are broken, and Max is afraid the horses will get out. Mark said he could be very late tonight."

"That's right, Jenny," I said. "Now I remember." Kyle nodded. Yes, that's why Mark wasn't there. He might not know exactly what was wrong but sensed the need to protect Mark.

"Well, I guess I'll see him tomorrow then," Lorelei said. "But Bobby. Where is Bobby? I need him for a special project."

"You know, Mommy," Kyle chimed in. "He went with Mrs. Benway."

"Oh. He hasn't come back?" We all shook our heads. No, Lorelei, he hasn't come back.

And may he never, I prayed.

"You children be sure to tell me when he does." Lorelei stood. "Now I must do some shopping. Without Mrs. Benway here, we must be low on food."

"We are," I said, "but what about Adam?" The others looked at me. Adam?

"You keep an eye on him, Kathryn. You're old enough. You're sixteen now."

"Oh, no, Mommy, I'm fourteen—fifteen soon on June 8, my homecoming day. But I know I can take care of Adam. I'll be very careful."

Subtracting several years from my age? I hoped I hadn't overdone it. She did a double take, shook her head slightly, and then smiled. "I know you will, dear. I will bring all of you chocolate chip cookies. Would you like that?"

We nodded yes, Mommy, and then she was gone.

"Who's Adam?" Jenny asked.

"Help me clean up, and I'll show you."

"I don't think we're going to like it." Staying at the ranch and just a few days of camp had changed Jenny. Suddenly, she seemed her age—twelve. This was good. I might need her help.

Baby Adam was awake and needed his diaper changed. Jenny found formula already mixed in a bottle, so we took him downstairs to feed him. None of us wanted to remain in Lorelei's bedroom. There wasn't space for all of us to sit. Besides, the room felt empty and dangerous.

Tomorrow was Thursday, I reminded them, the day of the big overnight. Jenny said she had packed already, so I urged the others to do so. Then Anna could bring Dusty back inside until bedtime. Kyle should take a bath, for he was the only one dirty beyond redemption. He complied, for once. He was tired and not much interested in the baby or the kitten.

I was alone with Adam and Jenny. "The sweet little thing," she said. "He's too young to be here, Kathy."

I agreed. "But I don't know what to do." Then I took a risk. "You seem to understand more than I realized, Jenny."

Jenny smiled. "I pretend a lot," she admitted. Then she spoke with a fake voice. "Your name is Jenny. Your name is Jenny. I am your mommy. You live here now. Your name is Jenny. Your name is Jenny." She looked into my eyes. "I remember that my name is really Janice. What's yours?"

I wrapped my arms around her. "It's Kitty," I said.

Adam drank his bottle and fell back asleep. Anna/Amy and Jenny/Janice played with Dusty the kitten. Kyle worked a simple jigsaw puzzle. Still, Lorelei did not return. Finally, we went upstairs. "Yes," I told Amy, "Dusty may stay in bed with you tonight." Amy understood that if all went as planned, this would be her last night with us. I put Adam back in his drawer bed. "I'll help you if I can," I whispered. Then I fell asleep and did not hear Lorelei come home.

June 5

Dear Kitty,

We arrived in Denver last night, earlier than expected, and checked into the dorm. I'll be rooming with Bob, a junior who's not as intimidating as the mighty seniors. Neither of us brought a lot of stuff, so we'll probably be okay in this small, basic room. No air conditioning, which means our room will become a towering inferno (really, we're on a top floor and Denver can be boiling in the summer), but the windows open, and I've heard it really cools down at night. Practically zero humidity, not at all like home. Tomorrow, we'll see the sights, including going to a folk concert at the Red Rocks Amphitheater. Accompanied by the famous Colorado sunset, it should be spectacular.

I saw a list of the resident apprentices on the student bulletin board in the cafeteria. Leesa Dulow at the bottom, written in pencil, so I guess she's a recent addition to the dorm. What luck, although finding her might be a needle-in-the-haystack situation. Hundreds are coming—most during the day tomorrow. We check in for classes and assignments on Friday. Shadowing Denver Post staff is just part of what we're doing. I'm still in shock at having this opportunity.

That bulletin board has given me an idea. There are folded messages on it already for various students. I got one myself, a welcome from a newspaper reporter who will be my mentor. I'm going to leave a simple one for Miss Dulow. Simple but clear enough, so she doesn't think I'm a dangerous stalker. Then, maybe I'll get an answer.

The odds of you being in Seguro Haven or even in Colorado are as remote as, well, Seguro Haven, Colorado. You disappeared seven years ago tomorrow. That day is almost a complete blur for me. The sorrowful days and angry months after are what I remember most.

Bob is growing impatient. Time to check out the food in this place. Probably just ordinary cafeteria food, but that's okay. I'm hungry. On the road, we subsisted on soda and chips.

Brother Tim

CHAPTER FIFTEEN

GAIN, I CAUTIONED THE CHILDREN to be quiet. They dressed, grabbed their overnight bags, and went down the back stairway.

Before following them, I peeked into Lorelei's room, just to make sure she had returned to Adam. Yes, the lump on the bed meant she was there asleep. All was quiet.

Because of everything going on in my head the night before, I was the one who hadn't packed. No matter. The children would fix their own breakfasts. Pajamas, hairbrush, a change of underwear and T-shirt, toothbrush and paste—I was ready. But I wasn't ready for what I faced in the kitchen— a pool of vomit and Jenny frantically using a kitchen towel to cover something on the floor. Kyle, looking stricken, entered from the downstairs bathroom. "It's Anna," he stage-whispered. "She's sick. She's throwing up. Can she still go to camp?"

Oh my God, no! She must! "Kyle, it will be all right. You go out and wait for the bus. If it comes early, tell the driver to wait. We'll be right there."

Kyle's eyes were wide, frightened. I patted him on the shoulder. "Please, Kyle," I said.

"All right, Kathy," he whispered, quietly opening the backdoor.

"I must go to Anna," I said. "But first, Jenny, what happened? I can tell you're hiding something."

Struggling to hold back tears, Jenny pointed to a half-full glass on the table. "When we came down, that was there. Anna drank a little and gave some to Dusty. We started fixing breakfast, but then she threw up and ran to the bathroom. Then Dusty started making funny sounds." Jenny gulped and began making her own funny sounds. Sobbing, she lifted the towel and showed me a tragic pile of gray fluff. "He's dead, Kathy."

I held up the glass and sniffed the thick, cloudy liquid. Buttermilk. Mark was the only one in the family who liked it. In fact, he loved it as much as the rest of us despised it. Evidently, Amy shared his taste. Lorelei had gone shopping, not just for cookies, but for buttermilk, poisoned especially for Mark. No wonder she needed Bobby.

I grabbed Jenny's arms. "Go be with Kyle," I ordered. "I'll help Anna. She must go, too. Convince the driver to wait if she doesn't join you before he comes."

"But this . . ." Jenny pointed to the messy vomit and sorrowful corpse.

"I'll take care of it and go to the church later." Six miles in all this heat, but I'd walk, if necessary.

Nodding, wiping her eyes, she re-covered the kitten. "Tell Anna I put Dusty back in the barn."

My precious sister! "Good girl," I said.

Amy was pale and miserable but had stopped vomiting. "Amy," I commanded, "you must go on the bus. Let's get you washed up the best we can. I'll give you some tablets to settle your stomach, but you must get outside fast. Don't let the driver get a good look at your face."

"I know, Kathy. I don't know what happened. I'm feeling a little better."

Well, she looked dreadful, but she might not be too noticeable by the time the bus reached the church—as long as she didn't throw up again. I grabbed a small tube of Tums from the cabinet and shooed her to the door. She turned back.

"What about Dusty?"

"Jenny took him back to Nelly. His mother will take care of him. Soon, yours will take care of you."

Fighting my own tears, I cleaned the mess and buried the kitten. I was about to throw away the buttermilk but stopped myself just in time. Instead, I took an empty Ball jar from a lower cabinet and poured and sealed the buttermilk. Then, wrapping it carefully in a kitchen towel, I added it to my bag.

What else before I left? I dashed off a quick note saying that tonight was the big camp overnight before the last day and that Mark and I were chaperones. Then I went to the barn and saddled up Firefly. It was time for him to make his home permanently with Mr. Tom on the Dulows' ranch. Checking first that Nelly had water, I poured some dry food into her bowl. She gave me a questioning meeow. "I know, Nelly. I am so sorry." Then I knelt down and kissed her sweet striped head. "I'll be back," I promised.

I had half hoped Leesa would still be there. We'd never really said goodbye. But if she had been, I would have had to explain why I wasn't at the camp. I'd never actually agreed to spend the day with them—just overnight—but taking the bus was to be my transportation into town. But Leesa and her father had left (he had decided to spend a few extra days in Denver). I didn't see Donna, and her car was gone.

Quickly, I transferred the personal items from the saddlebag into my overnight bag and made Firefly comfortable. She seemed pleased to see Mr. Tom again. Perhaps I'd bring Nelly and the kittens here, too. They'd be happier and better cared for. Then I noticed an envelope pinned to Firefly's stall. A note from Leesa, and inside was a key to her car!

Kath, sorry we didn't say goodbye, but we'll write, and I'll see you soon. I told Blanche she could borrow my car, once she returns from Idaho. When you get a chance, please drop the key into the Bennetts' mailbox; she expects it. Her parents will drive her out here to pick up the car. I don't want to leave the key hanging around with my family on vacation. Hope you and Mark have a great summer.

Love, Leesa

A great summer; I couldn't think past today. I wasn't even ready to handle thoughts of tonight. But a way into town had suddenly presented itself. Leesa had taught me how to drive, but did I dare? I would be very careful. The car was parked in its own small garage away from the main ones. I drove it out, then closed the door. Unlikely that Leesa's parents would even notice it was gone. The back road was deserted, no other car came along. Driving past the motel, I gave Mark a mental hug, wishing I could stop. Relieved, I finally pulled into Blanche's driveway, locked the car, and dropped the key into the mailbox. Then I walked the half-mile to the church grounds, joined the campers for a late morning snack, and let the rest of the day unfold.

Crafts, games, lunch, swimming, rest, songs, supper, preparing for sleeping in tents with blankets provided by church members—the day passed in a blur. Anna was a trooper, carrying on in spite of still feeling rotten. She fell sound asleep during the rest period.

Seven o'clock. Mark was graduating. Congratulations, Mark. I'm proud of you. I love you. Almost nine. It was time. I gave Amy a nudge, our agreed-upon signal.

"Kathy, I don't feel well. I think I'm going to throw up again."

"Ew!" was the helpful reaction of our tent mates.

"Come on, honey," I said. "I'll take you to the bathroom. I knew you'd eaten too many marshmallows. Take your bag along in case we have to call Mom to come get you."

That was our cover story, on this end at least. Kyle knew Amy had been sick, and Jenny would go along with whatever I said. She had learned. A few girls muttered that they hoped Anna would feel better, and we left to meet Mark.

He was waiting at the bus stop two short blocks from the church. The bus would travel to a main station in Delores, where they would transfer onto the late bus for Grand Junction, arriving early the next morning. I was certain Amy would sleep the whole way.

"Kathy," was all he said, before holding me briefly.

I didn't say anything because I was afraid I'd cry, but Amy threw her arms around me and did.

"Stop!" Mark said. "No tears. We don't want to give the bus driver any reason to question us. Here it comes. Kathy, go quickly so you aren't noticed. I will find you again."

I hid behind a tree and watched the bus take them out of my sight, and maybe out of my life. When I returned to the tent, everyone was asleep, but I lay awake for the rest of the night.

June 7

Dear Kitty,

Too busy to write yesterday. Everyone was determined to show us Denver. The concert and tour were terrific. Some of the boys say they would like to travel around the state before we go home in August. Boy, would I like that! If we can only figure out money and transportation. Well, for now, I'll be more than content with what I've got.

Breakfast is over, and we're about to go downstairs for the orientation, lasting until lunchtime. Then we'll have classes all afternoon. Our work at the newspaper won't start until Monday. Even then, it won't be all day. The paper can't have too many of us in the building, although I guess it's plenty big. Not like our tiny Galesburg Record. We will receive schedules, called shifts, and also have classes here. There will be lots of free time.

I left a note for Leesa Dulow, just saying that I'm trying to locate a relative who may live in Seguro Haven. That shouldn't scare her off—I hope. I wonder how long I'll have to wait for an answer—or if I'll even get one.

Notebook in hand, hair neat, cool black pants and a gray and white striped button-down shirt—I look as if I officially belong. Now I hope I can start feeling that way.

Wish me luck!
Tim

CHAPTER SIXTEEN

OTHER THAN A BRIEF REPRIMAND from the camp director—"You should always tell me if a camper is leaving early, dear"— no other comments were made about Amy. The tent mates had witnessed her sudden illness, and Kyle and Jenny knew enough to be quiet. Most of the children didn't even miss shy Anna, whom they hadn't known well, if at all.

Mark and Amy had reached Grand Junction by now, I thought, Amy reuniting with her family and Mark making his slow journey toward Flagstaff. I felt emptied, like a shell, carried along by strong forces I could no longer control.

We packed our gear completely before lunch, a simple sandwich affair, an easy clean up. Then we gathered around a bonfire, purely symbolic on this hot sunny Friday, and the counselors presented awards.

Kyle beamed at winning *Friendliest Camper*. Startled, I looked at him as if I'd never seen him before—never noticed that he was a person in his own right. And to think the majority of campers had voted for him! Yes, he was dear and friendly—remarkable considering what his life was like.

I had sensed that Jenny and Kara Dulow were on the outs. Kara glared daggers when Jenny was awarded *Most Helpful Camper* but relaxed some when she got *Best Song Leader*. Both girls were twelve and had been friends for a long time. No doubt squabbles at that age were normal; I wouldn't know. Then I remembered Blanche, who could have and should have been my friend. Maybe I did know something about jealousy.

Finally, we joined arms and sang closing goodbye songs. There were a few tears at our parting. I'd heard camp was like that.

The bus arrived, and we boarded for our six-mile ride home—but to what? What new problems and lies awaited us? I needed to come up with a believable explanation for Amy's absence. Jenny, seated next to me, must have had similar thoughts. "What are you going to tell Mommy about Anna? Where is she?" I just looked at her. "Oh, come on," Jenny said. "I know Mommy never came for her last night."

I was too tired and depressed for pat, instant answers. "Mark came and took Anna home to her parents. He's not coming back, either. I don't know what to tell Lorelei."

Jenny squeezed my hand. "Maybe you should tell the truth." But both of us knew that was a scary proposition. "I don't want to go back," she said.

I nodded. I didn't either.

At the ranch, Donna met the bus. Our house would be next—the last stop. Donna talked with the driver. I thought she was just thanking him, but then she said, "You Harris kids are getting off here, too."

Beyond relieved, not questioning yet, we followed Norm and Kara to the house, as the empty bus pulled away. Donna seemed determined about something, maybe even angry. "Where's Anna?" she asked suddenly.

Kyle answered. "Anna's real sick. Mommy took her home last night."

"Oh, is that the story?"

Kyle looked puzzled. That was the only explanation he knew.

Donna opened the kitchen door. "You kids freshen up and go play, but I need to talk privately with Kathryn."

Quietly but firmly, Jenny said, "I'm staying. I need to know what's going on."

Maybe she just didn't want to hang out with Kara, but . . . "She's old enough to be included," I said.

Donna nodded and led us into Mr. Dulow's study, where she didn't try to soften any blows. "Less than an hour ago I received a phone call from Mark—in Grand Junction. He's been arrested for kidnapping Anna!"

"No!" For the first time in my life, I fainted.

Not for long, it appeared, for I was aware of Donna waving something under my nose and trying to offer me water. Then I heard her say she would call Lorelei. "Even though Mark said—"

"Please, no!" Jenny's voice. "Don't call Mom . . . I mean, Lorelei. Mark didn't kidnap Anna. He took her home. Lorelei kidnapped Anna. She kidnapped all of us."

I reached out my hand to Jenny. Was I trying to stop her? Was I still trying to protect Lorelei? Habit, perhaps. "No," I said, managing to lift my head slightly. "Jenny's right. Don't call Lorelei. Call the police. Tell them to come here immediately." Wearily, I put my head down on the rug again. "We must think of Adam, too."

"Adam?" Donna shrieked.

"He's our new baby brother," Jenny said. "Lorelei brought him yesterday."

"Late Wednesday night," I corrected. "She said he was a newborn that she found in a dumpster. But he didn't look like a newborn to me. He's an infant, but he's older than that, and I thought he looked pretty healthy."

"Kathy named him Adam," Jenny added. "None of us have our real names anymore."

"Oh, dear God!" Donna rushed to the phone. She called the police, and then her husband.

With Jenny's help, I got myself to the couch, where we sat close together and did what we normally did—waited.

The Chief of Police and two officers accompanying him were skeptical at first. Who wouldn't be? "Poisoned buttermilk," one scoffed, until I brought out the Ball glass jar and suggested it be tested.

"She left it for Mark." Jenny began to cry. "He's the only one who likes buttermilk. Mommy didn't know Anna did, too." Jenny's use of the word Mommy was positively creepy. One of the officers shuddered. "It made Anna sick, and it killed her little kitten."

"Anna?"

"The girl Mark was accused of kidnapping," Donna explained.

"Only he was taking her home, and her real name is Amy," I said.

I told them about helping Georgia escape last summer, and then about Sarah and David. "We found their graves in the woods."

Donna turned on me. "Impossible! Lorelei is too small and frail. If you're telling the truth that they were murdered, someone else is guilty." Then she gasped. "Bobby?"

"Lorelei must have poisoned them. Bobby dug the holes and carried their bodies there. He didn't know better. He just said that when people died, he was in charge of burying them."

"Bobby is mentally handicapped, Chief Garland," Donna said. "Kathryn, how could you—"

"We'll sort this out later," the chief interrupted. "Carl, get out an APB for a" . . . he looked at his notes . . . "Margaret Benway and Herbert Benway. Randy, you remain here."

They were going to arrest Mrs. Benway? Well, she was in on everything. At least, she knew a whole lot. For Bobby's sake and because she did try to help us at the end, I hoped she wasn't found.

"And call Grand Junction and explain what you can. Then send some officers to arrest Lorelei Harris, if that's really her name."

It isn't, I thought, but I kept quiet. As he said, they'd sort it out. "Be careful of Adam," I said instead. Let Donna and Jenny explain. I was feeling woozy again, and sick to my stomach.

As Chief Garland and Officer Carl started to leave, though, I remembered something. "Adam will need formula, but I think Lorelei drugged his to make him sleep a lot."

Jenny nodded. "Yes, that's what she does."

"Dear God," Donna said again. "Perhaps you should take the baby to the hospital." The chief agreed. He would call someone to drive Adam to the one in Delores.

"Please, could you have someone bring Nelly and her two babies here where they'll be safe. I know you're busy, but please?"

"Jenny means the mother cat and two kittens in our barn," I said. The expression on the chief's face was almost comical.

He patted Jenny's head. "We'll make sure they're okay," he promised before leaving.

Officer Randy shuffled his feet, not quite sure what to do next. I was glad he would remain with us, though. Maybe he would help us feel safe.

Donna seemed to sense the man's uncertainty. "I should start supper," she said. "Would you like to come into the kitchen for a cup of coffee?"

"A Coke would be mighty nice, ma'am, but . . ." He looked at Jenny and me.

"You two must remain in the house," Donna said. "Kyle, too. And it might be a good idea for Kara and Norm."

"May I tell Kara what's happening?" Jenny asked. "She's my best friend, and I haven't liked keeping things from her."

Donna stared at me. Doubtless she was thinking of my best friend, Leesa, who knew nothing.

"I'll play with Kyle and Norm," I said quietly, not that I wanted to play anything with anyone but should try to make amends. Besides, there wasn't anything else to do but wait—for whatever would come next.

The boys were in Norm's bedroom—Norm glued to a Spiderman cartoon and Kyle fast asleep. I was not needed anywhere, and I was sick of waiting. Even though it wasn't smart, I wanted to see Lorelei, one more time before she was arrested. Hoping no one would stop me, I ran to the barn and saddled Firefly. With any luck, I'd get to the house ahead of the policemen.

Lorelei's van was parked out back. At least she hadn't left Adam alone. I heard noises coming from the living room. Yes, I was shaking with fear, but he was a helpless baby, more important than me.

"Lorelei," I said.

Pouting, she looked up from the bundle she cradled. "Kathryn," she scolded, "you know you are to call me Mommy."

I shook my head firmly. "I'm through pretending, Lorelei. Give me the baby."

"The baby, as you well know, is named Adam. Stop this nonsense at once! Or I'll . . ."

"Offer me some buttermilk?" This was not going well. I wondered if I had made a mistake in coming.

"Kathryn, what is wrong with you? This game of yours is not in the least bit amusing. You don't like buttermilk."

"No, I don't," I agreed, "but Mark does, and you know that. That's why you added poison. What kind? Arsenic? Rat poison?"

"Kathryn!" Lorelei screeched—the oddest scream I'd ever heard; not human—more like a wild, wounded animal. Adam began to wail. I was afraid she'd drop him, so I took him from her and put him on the couch. She didn't seem to notice.

At that point, two of us were crying—Adam and me. "Amy likes buttermilk, too, Lorelei," I screamed and sobbed at once. "So did her kitten. The kitten died, and Amy got sick. Mark didn't drink it—he took Amy to her real home. Did you poison David and Sarah, too, before you made Bobby bury them? It's over, Miss Josephine Grace Benway. Soon, everyone will know the truth!"

She lunged at me, hands outstretched, ready to choke away my life. Her mask had dropped, and while I wasn't certain the face I saw was evil, it certainly was twisted, insane. Normally, I was stronger than Lorelei, but at that moment, I wasn't sure. Both of us failed to see that we had been joined by three officers until two grabbed Lorelei's arms from behind.

"Lorelei Harris, aka Josephine Benway, you are under arrest for kidnapping, attempted homicide, and suspicion of homicide." The officer continued to read Lorelei her rights while she struggled and screamed. It took both officers to escort her to the waiting car.

I heard her last words in the distance. "I loved you, Kathryn."

"I loved you, too, Mommy," I whispered, before collapsing and crying my heart out.

"There, there." The policeman put an arm around me. "You'll be okay now." Gently, he lifted Adam from the couch. "I need to get this little mite to the hospital. Can you manage?"

I nodded. "I have my horse. I'll ride back to the ranch now. They'll be worried."

"The driver let them know you were here. It was foolhardy of you, but we heard every word, and it could be helpful." He started to leave. "Oh, be sure to tell the little girl that we won't forget her cat and kittens."

Back at the ranch, Donna just held me. I didn't say anything, nor did she.

Nothing about us would be decided that day. Chief Garland had called and talked with Donna. An officer would accompany Mark, flying from Grand Junction to Cortez, arriving late the next morning. Everyone still had a lot of questions. No kidding!

We were safe. I guess that's what mattered. It was Friday. A week ago, my whole life changed, and I had no idea what would come next. Oh, one more thing. By the time we fell into bed, Nelly and the kittens were also safe, with full stomachs, in the Dulows' barn with Firefly and Mr. Tom. All the animals had homes. Their people's fate was still to be determined.

June 7 (much later, same day)

Dear Kitty,

Orientation for those apprenticing at Denver Times was this morning. Not as large a group as I had anticipated—maybe thirty. Others have been assigned to different papers, both in Denver and surrounding areas. I think I was really lucky to get this post.

We heard from editors, reporters, mentors, and former apprentices—lots of interesting, exciting people, who seemed both anxious and willing to help us. All of them stressed the value of a free, diligent press to our democracy and how not all countries are as fortunate. It made me proud to be an American. We won't begin at the paper until Monday and will either be there or have classes here. The schedule will be posted at breakfast Monday morning.

I haven't met Leesa Dulow. She never responded to my note, although it is gone. Either she doesn't know anything or thinks I'm an idiot—or both. Maybe because of this, I did something I never expected to do. I told the orientation group about you. Really! After I vowed to go to a place where I wouldn't be known as the boy whose sister disappeared.

This is how it went. One of the teachers—at least, a man who will be giving classes—asked the group if any of us kept journals. I raised my hand and so did a few others. I was surprised that more hands weren't raised, and I guess the teacher was, too. He suggested that anyone who wanted to write should keep one. "There are many ways of going about it," he said, "and it doesn't have to be like a diary telling everything you do." Then he asked if any of us had a unique way of going about it, and this time I was the only one who raised my hand, so he called on me.

Suddenly, I wondered if Leesa Dulow might be in the room. Maybe this was a strange way I could finally introduce myself. I explained that my journal was mainly a series of letters that I had been writing since I was in fifth grade.

"To an imaginary person?" he asked.

"I don't know anymore," I said, puzzling everyone. Then I explained that my sister had disappeared from an airport seven years ago yesterday, when she was ten. "We never found out what happened to her, but my aunt thinks she might have been murdered because she was carrying an old brown leather Samsonite briefcase filled with money." I heard a gasp at that but couldn't tell where it came from. Leesa? Maybe, but what I said could have startled anyone. Then I chuckled and explained about the coincidence of finding out that Anne Frank wrote to an imaginary friend she called Kitty, and that my sister's name was Kitty. "Actually Katrina," I said.

The teacher wanted to know how writing the letters helped me, and things like that. Then another person asked a question, and my time was over. People approached me afterwards, saying my story was sad and interesting, but that's all that happened.

I'm waiting for Bob to return to the room, and then we'll decide if we want to join one of the parties in another room or just go to bed. Lots of area trips planned for the weekend—Pike's Peak, The Garden of the Gods, a real gold mine. As intriguing as it all sounds, I would rather it be Monday so we can get to work.

Bob just came back. He does want to go to a party but doesn't think I will—"once you read this"—he informed me mysteriously, before handing me a note. "She's cute. Stay out of trouble."

Get this! Leesa Dulow wants to meet me right away in the canteen. She thinks we might have something in common. Could be about anything, but maybe it's about you, Kitty.

Fingers crossed!
Tim

"Y OUR EYES LOOK DIFFERENT TODAY," Officer Randy said the next morning. "They're blue. I could have sworn—"

"Yes," I said. "I wear brown contacts to disguise my blue eyes. They're not prescription—I see okay—but my eyes get sore so I decided not to wear them, now that . . ." He looked shaken, as if he couldn't quite believe the lengths Lorelei had gone to strip us of our identities.

More policemen arrived, as well as a detective and a few reporters, shooed away after being promised a later update. It was going to be another hard day. I wondered how long I'd be stuck on Donna's living room sofa, Jenny and Kyle clinging to either side of me. When no one was looking, each of them handed me a homemade card. "Happy Homecoming Day, Kathy!" I managed not to cry. June 8—I was officially seventeen, although I had actually been so since March 22. "Thank you," I whispered, hugging both of them, before the detective pulled over a chair to face us.

He said that most likely I'd be called to testify at Lorelei's trial—something I really didn't want to do. Then he advised me not to say anything to the press and to get a lawyer. "I'm just a kid," I wanted to say. "What would I know about getting a lawyer?"

The detective's mission was to figure out where we children belonged. I was able to help the most. I gave him my real name, address in Galesburg, Illinois, and our old phone number. "I have no idea if my aunt and brother still live there," I said. The detective tried the number, but there was no answer and no answering machine. He would keep on trying.

"There are ways of finding people," he bragged. I didn't point out that no one had been successful at finding me—or the others.

Jenny didn't remember as much, but she was only eight when she arrived. "My name is Janice," she said. "Janice Barber. I lived in California, but we were moving. I don't know where. My parents stopped at a gas station and told me to wait in the car. But I got tired of waiting, so I got out. That's all I remember." Probably she was enticed into Lorelei's van and drugged. It was unlikely she'd ever recall. Just as well, I thought.

Then it was Kyle's turn. He was only three or so when he joined the Harris family. We had explained a little the night before—just enough so he wouldn't be frightened. I had convinced the detective that it would be best if I questioned Kyle first, although he would stay to witness. Kara insisted on being at Jenny's side—that friendship might be firmer now than Leesa's and mine.

"Kyle," I said, holding him close. "You know that we all had different names before we became Harris children, right?"

He nodded. "Anna used to be Amy," he said.

"That's right. You call me Kathy, but my real name is Kitty." Although I knew I would never go back to that name. "Mark used to be Matthew, and Jenny was Janice. I know it was a long time ago. You weren't even four when you came here. But do you remember if you ever had another name? Did grownups and friends call you something else?"

Kyle sat quietly in thought. Then he said, "Kenny. Kenny J. There was a Kenny B. but I was Kenny J."

Stupidly, the detective interrupted. "What I don't understand is why you kids never told anyone? How could you have kept quiet for so long?"

Kyle stood suddenly and began to chant in a strange voice: *Your name is Kyle. Your name is Kyle. I am your mommy. Your name is Kyle. I am your mommy. Please let me out, Mommy. I'll be good. My name is Kyle, you are my mommy, my name is Kyle . . .* He began sobbing hysterically. Donna rushed over to gather him into her arms.

"Satisfied?" asked an angry male voice. "It's called brainwashing. She locked us up, drugged us, and repeated our new names over and over. That's why we never told. We were scared."

"Mark!" I yelled, throwing myself into his arms.

"It's okay, Kathy. We'll be all right now." He held me tightly, and I could tell he had been every bit as frightened as I.

The detective, who was kind of sheepish and apologetic after Kyle's outburst, suddenly remembered a cold case in Jackson Hole, Wyoming. A three-year-old boy had been taken from a daycare program. Kyle might have been called Kenny J. because there was a Kenny B. in his class.

Again, Officer Randy stayed, although he seemed uncertain what to do. Donna insisted that Mark eat. Sometimes, feeding people was all grownups knew how to do when things were complicated. The rest of us decided, though, that we were hungry and joined Mark. We weren't really, but sometimes nervousness feels like hunger.

Later, Mark and I rode to Curtain Call Gap. Mr. Tom was excited to see Mark and neighed the entire time he was being saddled. Firefly was calmer but seemed pleased that the four of us were reunited. The horses enjoyed apples and sweet grass while Mark and I sat on the edge of the cliff and gazed at the San Juans—mountains that had become a part of us.

"Were you scared?" I asked.

"Terrified," he admitted. "No one was home, so I took Amy to the police station. I couldn't just leave her there, so we went inside. They didn't believe her story, and neither did her parents when the police tracked them down. I was afraid to call the house, so I took a chance on Donna."

"Good thing." I explained how Donna took all of us off the bus when it reached the ranch. Then I told Mark about Adam and about my final confrontation with Lorelei.

He held me close. "Oh, Kathy, it was never going to stop."

"Never. She wasn't all bad, Mark. How could I love someone who did such bad things? I don't understand why she did it."

"How can you understand crazy?"

I nodded, overwhelmed. In time, I found out the answer. I learned what had led to Lorelei's mental breakdown, but I didn't know anything when Mark and I sat on the cliff, contemplating our future. "What's going to happen to us?"

"What would you like to happen to you, Kathy?"

I gazed down at the stream far below, and then high up at Delores Peak, way in the distance. It was never the same. The lights of morning, noon, night, summer, fall, winter, spring, always presented a different spectacular view. How could I leave? Finally, I answered Mark. "I want to stay here always, but I don't suppose I'll be allowed to."

"At Lorelei's house? I don't think I could ever go back there."

"I could, although I'd prefer the ranch. I won't be able to stay at either place. The Dulows won't want me after all the lies. I'm a minor, so I guess I'll go wherever I'm sent."

Mark nodded. "Well, you won't be a minor forever."

"What about you, Mark? You're not one."

"I'd like to come back here occasionally," he said. "We'll see. For now, I'll just carry on with my plans. At least the police have enough information to find my actual birth certificate. I'll still go to Flagstaff, but probably I'll have to stay for the trial first.

"I don't want to lose Jenny or Kyle—or you."

We were quiet after that. There wasn't much else to say.

It was late afternoon when we rode back to the ranch—in silence. Mr. Dulow's car was parked in front, so I guess we'd face additional questions, although I hoped Donna had filled him in. Avoiding the inevitable, stalling for time, we checked on Nelly and the kittens, cooled off Firefly and Mr. Tom, giving them thanks, compliments, and loving pats, and then braced ourselves for what awaited us in the house.

Several people were in the living room, but the one I saw first was Leesa. I stayed back, shy, certain that I no longer deserved her friendship. But she grabbed me into a hug. "It's all right, Kath. I understand. Come, I want you to meet someone. A new friend I met in Denver."

Curious, I followed her. A boy stood as we approached the sofa. He seemed a little young for Leesa. Cute, tall, with sandy-colored curly hair—smiling a half-smile, perhaps a little shy, too. Then I looked into his eyes—bright blue and familiar. I knew this boy.

"Hello, Tim," I said.

THREE YEARS LATER, I'M STILL trying to put it all together. Some things I may never know—even if investigators do—such as the true identities of David and Sarah or what became of Georgia, the Benways, and Bobby.

I suppose the reason I'm writing about my unusual life is because Tim shared his journal with me—all those "Dear Kitty" letters he wrote throughout the years. After reading them and hearing the families' stories before Lorelei's sentencing, I realized how selfish I'd been back then, never really considering what other people were going through. It took a long time to take a hard look at myself—to be able to accept my share of the blame.

The trials were terrible, although I didn't have to attend many. A lot of our information was taken by deposition. Mark and I spent the rest of June and July at the ranch, thanks to the Dulows, who cancelled their own vacation. (Leesa and Tim returned to Denver for their apprenticeships at the newspaper.) In August, after Tim's tour of the state with friends, he and I returned to Aunt Kay in Galesburg, and Mark left for the university. Jenny's and Kyle's parents were located, as well as baby Adam's. I doubt that I'll ever see my pretend siblings again. Their parents seemed pretty firm about that. It makes me unhappy, so I try not to think about it.

The only time I had to face Lorelei was at her sentencing later in the year when I returned to Colorado. The parents stood and told Lorelei what she had done to them. The hardest person for me to listen to was a fifteen-year-old girl named Abby, who had been Adam's (Theo's) babysitter in the town of Fruita. Abby had been about to take Theo for a walk when she noticed she'd left her cell phone in the house. Leaving him in the stroller in his parents' front yard, she zipped inside to get it. There, her boyfriend called, and she answered. Yes, they probably talked a little too long, but Theo had seemed content and safe enough. When she returned, the stroller was there, but Theo was gone. In court, Abby was crying so hard she could hardly speak. "Everyone hates me now," she said. "No one will ever trust me again!" I cried, too. Lorelei had hurt everyone—they all had heartbreaking tales— but Abby's got to me the most. I understood then that it's possible to do something that seems harmless, only to have it turn into something dreadful. Something you have to live with.

Mark and I were invited to speak, too, but he refused. He figured that up until the time she decided to kill him, Lorelei had done him a favor. The detectives found his stepfather, who said that unless there was money in it, he didn't want anything to do with Mark.

I couldn't say anything, either. But before Lorelei was led off to serve a life sentence, we gazed at each other. I saw and felt love again. That old question that haunts me and is never answered returned. How can you love someone who does bad things? I wonder if I'll ever know.

We did find out what had happened to Lorelei back when she was Josephine Benway. She was married with three children and then divorced. One night, she went to a neighbor's house, leaving Bobby and the two younger children alone and, she thought, sound asleep. The little boy started playing with matches, the curtains caught fire, and then the house as well. Both children burned to death while Bobby went frantically from neighbor to neighbor searching for his mother. I wondered if it had really been the little boy's fault. Matches had fascinated Bobby. The tragedy would explain a lot about Lorelei's mental problems.

Mark and I could have saved the court the trouble of trials and sentencing if they'd listened to us in the first place. Lorelei went completely berserk in prison and was transferred to a facility for the hopelessly insane. As guilty as hell—but for reasons of insanity.

Galesburg never worked out for me. Although she won't admit it, Aunt Kay won't ever forgive me for going willingly with Lorelei. She is only biding her time until Tim graduates and she is able to return to her sister in Detroit.

Lisa Manion and I were unable to resume our friendship; she had her popular friends—I was a short-term curiosity. Tim had his friends, too, but I had no one. If I sound sorry for myself, well, okay, that's the way it was. I was so far behind it took two more years for me to finish high school. Tim is a senior now, even though he's so much younger than I.

Leesa is doing great, and we text and Skype often. She's studying at NYU, still planning on a journalism career. I'm envious but also very proud of her. And then there's Mark. Yes, we're still close. He's finishing up in Flagstaff. We phone and make plans to get together—plans that are never realized. It's funny, though. We're more like brother and sister now than we ever were at Lorelei's. I seem to need family more than . . . well, you know.

Have I changed? Not as much as you might think. There's still a secretive side to me, deeply ingrained, no doubt. For instance, I kept the money. No one ever asked about it, so I never said anything. Probably Aunt Kay thought Lorelei took it. But it's in the bank now—not in a briefcase or saddlebag—so that's an improvement.

I've just started my degree in Equine Studies at Colorado State University in Fort Collins. My roommate is Blanche Bennett, but that's another story.

BACKSTORY

ONCE LONG AGO, I SPENT time in the waiting room of Grand Junction's Walker Field, now named Grand Junction Regional Airport, where I noticed a young girl playing string games and Mad Libs all by herself. Her mother left her alone for a few minutes, and I struck up a conversation, even showed her a few of my own special string tricks. After "Mom" returned and they left, I scribbled a note in my journal and didn't look at again for years when I was searching for something new to write. What if? I wondered. What if—I suppose that's how all stories begin.

Somewhere between hither and yon, in the real San Juan National Forest, lies the fictitious, clueless community of Seguro Haven, Colorado, located within driving distance—weather permitting—of the real towns, Delores, Cortez, and Durango. Seguro Haven is not, alas, the safe place one might expect for the fictional characters of the young adult novel, *Waiting Games.*

W AITING GAMES IS MARILYN LUDWIG'S ninth novel, the third located in Western and Southwestern Colorado, where she spent her early childhood. She has lived in Downers Grove, Illinois for forty-seven years and is a member of the Society of Children's Book Writers and Illustrators (SCBWI).